DANGER—
HIGH EXPLOSIVES

—read the sign on the powder house door. "Guess I better have a look-see," said Slade, as he made his evening round. "Things have been a mite too quiet. . . ."

Drawing near he sensed a flicker of moving shadow, and suddenly saw a flash of bright flame—crawling slowly, silently toward the arsenal. Slade bounded forward, scooped up the bundle of dynamite—with the sputtering fuse attached—and groped for his pocket knife . . . but it wasn't there!

Gripping the fuse between his teeth, Slade chewed frantically, sparks creeping close to his face. He gasped, enduring the agony of the burns as the flames seared his mouth, and in one last grinding effort he realized that he still held the lethal bundle intact . . . **with scarcely an inch of smoking fuse remaining! !**

GUNSIGHT SHOWDOWN

BRADFORD SCOTT

WILDSIDE PRESS

First Printing, November 1962

ONE

FROM WHERE RANGER WALT SLADE, whom the Mexican *peones* of the Rio Grande river villages named *El Halcón*—The Hawk—sat his tall black horse, the vista was as of some raw planet in its earliest and wildest state, rather than of the homely earth.

Behind him were the silver mines of Shafter, and hidden trails frequented by smugglers and raiding bandit gangs. To the left, the rugged Cienaga Mountains. Mesquite, creosote, sagebrush, and bunch grass grew on the floor of the narrow valley of Cibolo Creek which he had traversed, with, higher up on the slopes, the eternal green of the piñon and juniper blending into the soft haze of thickets and oaks. Here the trail skirted the foothills of the Chinati Mountains to the west to drop over the cap rock.

The transition was startlingly abrupt. On the tableland he had just passed over were grass and timbered slopes. Then suddenly the heights slid away, in a rubble of debris, to the edge of a stark desert hundreds of feet below. On this dead expanse the sun beat down with a scorching, dazzling heat, reflected blindingly from the gleaming sands. On the rock-strewn desert there was no shade and no vegetation other than cactus, sage, and the ghostly snake-like arms of the ocotillo.

Like to a country of burned marl extending forever.

But man was there. The blazing sun shone down on his handiwork. Paralleling southward were twin steel ribbons, shimmering, hovered over by dancing heat waves. And against the southern horizon was a dark smudge staining the clear blue of the sky. Which marked, Slade knew, a great railroad construction camp.

And in the nearer distance was a long line of crawling dots —one of the cart trains that carried goods from Mexico via the Chihuahua Trail to the Old Spanish Trail which, east and west, traversed the breadth of Texas.

"Well, Shadow, guess we'd better be moving," Slade told his horse. "Sun's low in the sky and will be behind the mountains before long; but we should be able to make it to the construction camp by a little after dark, where I figure there's a chance for us both to put on the nosebag. Then, if we can't tie onto a place to sleep, we'll go on to Presidio, where I'm pretty sure we can. Let's go."

Shadow skated and slithered down the slope, his snorts

undoubtedly equine profanity expressing his opinion of such rough going. However, he reached the desert floor without mishap.

Here, late in the day though it was, the heat was withering, the dazzle of the sands hard on the eyes; but both horse and rider were accustomed to such terrains and paid little mind to its discomforts.

As he rode, Slade watched the vehicles of the cart train grow larger and larger. Before long he would meet them. He shook his head as they drew near. Their route paralleled the railroad right-of-way, the rival that would doom or at least greatly reduce their lucrative activities. For hundreds of years the cart trains had been the sole means of transportation from the south and vice versa.

As the foremost vehicle of the train reached him, Walt Slade got a surprise. He had expected the carters to be Mexicans, but they definitely were not. They were hard-eyed, alert looking men who showed no indications of Spanish or *Indio* blood. They nodded shortly to the lone horseman, swept a searching gaze over him, then faced to the front. Slade waited until the train had creaked and rumbled past, then resumed his southward course.

"That's a funny one, Shadow," he remarked. "We've been down in this section several times and this is the first time I've seen carters who weren't Mexicans. Those gents certainly were not. Salty looking jiggers, too, and they sure gave us a thorough once-over, although not seeming to do so. Wonder what's the meaning of it? May be a tie-up with the reason for us being here. I wonder, now."

After riding a little distance, he halted Shadow and gazed back at the cart train, now dwindling away into the northern distance.

He made a striking picture against the flame of the sunset. Very tall, more than six feet, with broad shoulders and a well-developed chest which slimmed down to a lean, sinewy waist. His bronzed face was dominated by rather large eyes of a very pale gray—cold, reckless eyes that nevertheless always seemed to have little devils of laughter lurking in their clear depths, devils that, if occasion warranted, leaping to the fore, could be anything but laughing.

His rather wide mouth, grin-quirked at the corners, relieved somewhat the sternness, almost fierceness evinced by the prominent hawk nose above, and the powerful jaw and chin beneath. His pushed-back "J.B." revealed thick, crisp hair, so black that a blue shadow seemed to lie upon it.

Slade wore the simple, efficient garb of the rangeland with

the careless grace with which the Conquistadores wore steel. Bibless overalls, soft blue shirt with a vivid neckerchief at the throat, well scuffed half-boots of softly tanned leather and the broad-brimmed, neatly creased and dimpled rainshed.

Around his waist were double cartridge belts, with carefully worked and oiled cut-out holsters from which protruded the plain black butts of heavy guns.

And from the butts of those big Colts his slender, powerful hands seemed never far away.

Shadow, the horse, was a fitting mount for his rider. Nearly eighteen hands high, his satiny coat was black as a starless night. His body was long, his legs slender rods of steel. His glorious mane was a black ripple that caught the light. His eyes were large and liquid, filled with fire and intelligence. His lines bespoke not only speed but great endurance.

A picture to catch the eye, and hold it, a gallant man on a gallant horse.

Slade watched the retreating cart train for a moment, then, with a shrug of his shoulders, turned his face to the south and spoke to Shadow, who ambled along over the hot sands.

El Halcón would have been interested in the conversation taking place between the drivers of the two rearmost carts.

"Who the devil is that big ice-eyed hellion, I wonder?" one remarked.

"Chuck-line-riding cowhand, the chances are," returned his companion.

"Maybe. Sort of dresses like one, but somehow he don't look like one."

The other shrugged. "Looks, too, like a gent with places to go. Mexico ain't far off and sometimes his sort find it convenient to put the Rio Grande between them and Texas."

"Uh-huh," the first speaker admitted, "but somehow he don't look like that sort to me, either; not the runnin' sort. Wish I could get him outa my mind. Somehow he bothers me. Hey, now what?" he exclaimed, glancing ahead.

Midway along the line a cart had pulled out and come to a halt. The driver held his position until the rear cart was abreast of him.

"What's the matter?" asked the driver of the rearmost cart.

"Oh, nothing," the halted driver replied as he spoke to his

7

mules, and the cart moved on. "Nothing, except I figured you might be wondering about that feller we just passed."

"Was talking about him," the other conceded.

"Don't know who he is, Clate?"

"Never saw him before," Clate replied.

"And if you never see him again it'll be soon enough," said the driver. "Clate, the big jigger is El Halcón."

"What!"

"Gives you a bit of a start, eh? Figured it would. Yep, he's El Halcón. I recognized him the minute I clapped eyes on him. I saw him once before, and once you see him you don't forget him, especially if he happens to be looking over gunsights at the time."

"Blount, are you sure?" Clate asked.

"Of course I'm sure!" Blount snorted. "You think I could make a mistake with him or that horse?"

Clate muttered profanity. "I wonder what the devil he's doing here?" he growled.

"Hard to tell," said Blount. "But wherever he shows up, trouble busts loose. You know his reputation for hornin' in on the good things other folks have got started."

Clate swore some more. "Well," he declared viciously, "a bullet can stop him same as anybody else."

"Uh-huh," Blount agreed dryly, "but I'd advise you not to try it, at least not when he's looking your way, and he seems to have eyes in the back of his head. Guess you've heard what folks say about him—the 'singingest man in the whole Southwest, with the fastest gunhand.' I figure both to be gospel truth."

Clate swore again, with added fervor. "As if I didn't have enough on my hands, running this infernal train and trying to keep you work dodgers outa ruckuses!" he growled. "*Why* is he here?"

"Maybe old Jaggers Dunn, who runs the blasted C. & P. Railroad, brought him in," Blount suggested. "He's sure got the look of a professional gun-slinger."

"Maybe, but I doubt it," said Clate. "Dunn is a salty old cuss, but he never struck me as the sort that'd hire a paid gun to do his fighting for him."

Blount nodded. "And I gotta admit El Halcón don't strike me as the hired gun type," he admitted. "Sure wish I knew just what he is; nobody ever seems to be sure." He turned on the cart seat and gazed south.

"He's headed for the construction camp, I'll bet a hatful of *pesos*," he said. "At the rate he was going he's liable to be

8

just right to run into something there. And if he does, the devil only knows what he'll pull off."

"That's what's got me bothered most," said Clate. "Well, anyhow, the Boss has gotta hear about this right away."

"He's liable to hear about it faster than we can tell him and not particularly enjoy the hearing," was Blount's consoling remark.

"Oh, shut up!" yelped Clate. "Get in line ahead of us and forget about the hellion for a while. Give me a chance to think."

Blount, who apparently enjoyed getting the cart train boss riled, concealed a grin and obeyed.

TWO

THE SUN VANISHED behind the Chinatis in a splendor of scarlet and gold. The lovely blue dusk began sifting down from the hilltops and the heat diminished appreciably. Slade rode on, gazing expectantly to the south.

Low down appeared "echoes" of the stars blossoming in the darkening sky—the lights of the construction camp. Slade quickened Shadow's gait a little. The black horse· sniffing oats in the offing, made no objection. Slade relaxed comfortably in the saddle. "Another twenty minutes or so and we'll make it," he said.

Abruptly he straightened up, staring. The whole southern sky was ablaze with yellowish light. Moments later a rumbling boom reached the Ranger's ears.

"What in blazes!" he wondered. "If that was a dynamite explosion, it sure wasn't set properly, making all that light. Get going, horse, I've a notion something isn't as it ought to be down there."

Shadow lengthened his stride still more. Slade peered ahead. A little later his hand tightened on the bridle.

In the gloom ahead had materialized shapes, grotesque, unreal. They quickly resolved to five speeding horsemen. Slade's eyes narrowed a trifle.

"I don't know what this is all about, but I figure it's a good notion to give those hurrying gents the right of way," he muttered.

Not far from the trail was a big ocotillo brandishing its snaky arms. Slade swerved his mount and halted him in its shadow, which did not provide much concealment.

On came the riders. Now they were opposite where the Ranger sat his horse. He saw the white blur of faces turned in his direction, saw a sudden gleam of shifting metal. He was already sideways out of the saddle as a gun blaze and a slug yelled through the space his body had occupied an instant before.

Walt Slade didn't take kindly to being shot at for no apparent good reason. He signified his dissent in no uncertain terms. Prone on the ground and in the deeper shadow, he whipped both guns from their sheaths and sent a stream of lead hissing in reply.

A yell of pain echoed the reports, and another. He saw one of the riders slump forward and grab the saddle horn to

10

keep from falling. A second lurched sideways, recovered, sagging in the hull.

The bunch did not pause to try conclusions with him, hidden in the shadow as he was. They tore on up the trail, two of them reeling and swaying but keeping their seats.

Slade leaped to his feet, slid his heavy Winchester from the saddle boot, then changed his mind and resheathed the long gun. After all, the bunch might be but a band of trigger-nervous cowhands who had been startled by the apparition of the horseman lurking in the shadow of the big candlewood. This was a wild land, and such a one might well be suspect. He muttered wrathfully and glared after the vanishing riders.

Later he was to regret that he changed his mind and replaced the rifle without using it.

"Let's go, horse," he said as he forked Shadow. "This is beginning to turn out to be something of a night. Bet you we find more trouble at the camp—I've got a feeling."

Twenty minutes later they reached the outskirts of the big construction camp, which was in an uproar, men shouting and cursing and bawling orders. A locomotive lay on its side, spouting steam from broken pipes. A big crane also lay slanted sideways, half in and half out of a hole hollowed in the ground near the tracks of a siding. A boxcar was roofless, another had been turned at right angles to the tracks. Still another was a mass of tangled wreckage strewn over the ground. Around this last was a swirl of activity. Just beyond it, spike mauls were thudding frantically as a crew laid a line of rails parrallel to the wreckage. On these rails stood another and heavier crane, with a hissing locomotive shoving it along as fast as the track layers could place the iron.

From where he sat his horse Slade could see over the heads of the crowd to where workmen were swarming like distrubed ants over the wreckage.

In the forefront, directing operations, was a broad-shouldered, stocky but powerfully built individual with craggy features, keen blue eyes and a glorious crinkly white mane sweeping back from his big, dome-like forehead. It was James G. "Jaggers" Dunn, the famous General Manager of the great C. & P. Railroad system. His voice boomed orders liberally spiced with profanity.

Slade dismounted, shouldered his way through the crowd and touched Dunn on the arm. The G.M. whirled around with an exasperated exclamation. Then his eyes widened and he stared.

"Slade!" he exploded. "Where the devil did *you* come from?"

11

"Tell you later," Slade replied. "What's going on here?"

"Some blankety-blank-blanks set off a charge of dynamite and blew up half the camp," Dunn answered. "Tell *you* about *that*, later. Right now I've got trouble on my hands. There's a poor devil of a workman pinned under that mess. A heavy beam, a side sill, is resting across his chest and holding him. The beam is slowly pressing down on him as the ends of the sill, resting on other timbers and weighted with wreckage, sinks as the wreckage beneath it settles into the soft earth. We're trying to get the big hook over there into position where it can lift the wreckage off the beam, and the boys are laying track as fast as they can to accommodate it, but I'm afraid we won't make it in time. The poor hellion will be crushed to death before we can raise the stuff. That crack in the wreckage is so narrow only one man can crawl in there and he can't do anything but try and comfort him."

Slade squatted down and peered down the narrow aperture between the splintered timbers.

"Get that fellow out of there," he told Dunn. "Hurry!"

The General Manager bawled an order. The workman came shuffling back out of the crack. Slade moved forward and peered. By the light of the flares blazing on all sides he could make out the form of the pinned man. He could also see that on one side of his body the beam was lifted a couple of feet from the earth. He turned to Dunn.

"A shovel, quick!" he said.

The G.M., who knew Slade well and had experience with his handling of what appeared a hopeless situation, obeyed the order without question. Trailing the shovel after him, Slade wormed his way into the opening and began scooping out the earth in the shallow hollow under the beam.

The pinned man was moaning softly, but was still conscious.

"Take it easy," Slade told him. "Don't try to breathe too hard. Relax your muscles and don't try to fight that thing. We'll get you out."

The calm, steady voice had the desired effect. The fellow calmed, the wild look left his eyes and was replaced by one of confidence.

"Guess if you say it's so, it is," he panted. Slade scooped frantically at the earth under the beam.

"That ought to do it," he muttered, pushing the shovel aside. He crawled into the deepened hollow, braced himself on hands and knees and raised his back until it came in contact with the sinking beam.

At first the weight was nothing, but slowly and steadily it increased, until the strain on his arms and legs was terrific.

12

He could feel the wood grinding into his flesh and he began to breathe heavily. An iron band seemed to be tightening and tightening around his chest. His eyes bulged, his temples throbbed. The terrible pressure was almost more than he could bear, but—

The beam had stopped sinking!

A face appeared in the opening, the face of General Manager Dunn.

"How you doing?" he asked hoarsely.

"Okay so far," Slade panted. "Don't know how long I can hold out."

"The hook's almost in position," Dunn said. "A little more and we'll be ripping that stuff off. Once we get the trucks that are on top of the wood off the weight will ease. Just a few minutes more."

Outside a voice suddenly bawled, "Mr. Dunn! Mr. Dunn! that blankety-blanked stuff's on fire!"

Bellowing profanity, Jaggers Dunn went shuffling back out of the hole. Another moment and his voice was roaring orders.

Now smoke was filtering through the chinks in the wreckage. Slade gasped and coughed. Bands of light were flickering past his eyes, then coils of blackness. Already the heat was intense, and above he could hear the crackling of the flames eating into the oil soaked wood. The pinned man began gibbering with fright.

"Easy!" Slade panted. "Save your strength. They'll make it."

The poor devil quieted. Slade wondered if they *would* make it. His muscles, bulging on arms and shoulders, were turning to water. A little more and he would collapse, which would very likely mean the finish for both of them. The ringing spike mauls were like the measured tolling of a passing bell.

Suddenly they ceased. He heard the boom of the locomotive's exhaust, the grinding of steel on steel. The exhaust ceased. There was a creaking and jangling. Voices hummed and murmured overhead. The creaking grew louder, culminated in a ripping crash. Again, and yet again. Slade braced himself and summoned his last reserve of strength for a final effort.

Abruptly the crushing weight on his back lessened. He heard the crash of tossed-aside iron and timber, as the crane's beam swung around and dropped its load, and swung back for more. The jangling of chains, a scratching and scraping as of a horde of giant rats. The chatter of the engine and the intolerable pressure on his back almost ceased. One more

13

rending crash. One more back swing of the crane arm. Another creak and crash and the relief was so great he almost fainted.

"We've got the beam!" Jaggers Dunn roared. "Easy, now, easy. Hold it! Crawl out, Slade, we've got it!"

Slowly, carefully, fearful that there still might be some mistake, El Halcón eased down. Above him the beam hung motionless. He wormed his way to the near unconscious worker, gripped his shoulders and hauled him free. Another moment and he was shuffling backward through choking smoke and blistering heat, dragging the rescued man after him.

Light blazing against his eyes! A gulping draught of sweet, fresh air. Then hands gripping him, hauling him and his burden away from the burning wreckage. Old Jim Dunn peering with anxious eyes.

"You all right?" he choked.

"Fine as frog hair," Slade replied, smiling wanly. "Was touch and go, though. If you fellows hadn't rattled your hocks out there I'm afraid we would have both been goners. Give me a hand, will you?"

Dunn's huge paw lifted him erect and supported him until he was steady on his feet. Others were ministering to the rescued workman who was sore and cut and bruised but apparently had suffered no serious injury. He held up a hand to Slade.

"Much obliged, feller, I won't forget it," he croaked. Slade patted him on the shoulder.

A hose line had been hooked up to the locomotive and the fire was being quenched.

"Was afraid to risk it until we got you out, for fear we'd scald you," Dunn observed to Slade. "Don't know how the devil it caught. Must have been a spark from the explosion smoldering in there somewhere. Wind fanned it and that grease-smeared mess flared up like a grass fire. Began to look like you'd be cooked as well as squashed. Okay, come on over to the car. I've a notion some hot coffee and a bite to eat ought to set well with you about now."

"First my horse," Slade said. "Then it'll go fine."

Dunn let out a bellow and a man came running, who was properly introduced to Shadow, after which the big black allowed himself to be led to a leanto where other critters were accommodated. First Slade secured his rifle and saddle pouches. Then he and the G.M. made their way to a long, green and gold splendor with WINONA stencilled on the

14

sides, that sat on a nearby siding; General Manager Dunn's palatial private car.

"You remember Sam, don't you?" said Dunn as they clambered aboard. "He's still with me."

"Quite well," Slade replied and shook hands with the smiling colored man who met them at the door.

"Fine to have you back with us, Mistuh Walt," said Sam, and hurried off to prepare a meal.

THREE

THE PRIVATE CAR, along with about every other convenience, boasted a tiny bathroom where Slade cleaned up to his satisfaction. After which he rejoined Dunn in the sittingroom of the coach.

"And now suppose you tell me what it was all about?" he suggested as he sat down and rolled a cigarette.

"An example of the harrassment to which I've been subjected ever since I started this blasted feeder which will eventually reach Chihuahua City," Dunn growled. "Some hellion or hellions slid into the working force, which wasn't hard to do—I have hundreds of men working on the line."

"Five in number, I'd say," Slade interpolated.

"What the devil do you mean by that?" Dunn demanded. Slade recounted his brush with the five night riders.

"I made a mistake in not throwing down on them with my saddle gun, but right then I didn't know what they'd been up to," he concluded. "Go on."

"Yes, I guess those were the devils," Dunn nodded. "They did a pretty good job with their dynamite blast. Smashed a locomotive, a crane and those boxcars. A plain wonder that they didn't kill somebody. They would have if it wasn't for you. I wouldn't have believed there was a man in Texas who could stop that beam from sinking; but then, you're always doing something nobody figures could be done.

"Well, as I was saying, I've been having trouble a-plenty. This isn't the first incident. Had a couple of very suspicious fires, telegraph lines cut, a few shootings from the brush that scared the devil out of the workers, even though nobody was hit. Keeps 'em fumbly and jerky and slows up progress. Tonight was about the most ambitious try of all."

"Who's back of it?" Slade asked. Dunn shrugged his massive shoulders.

"Not easy to answer," he replied. "I have opposition from the carters, who see the line cutting in on their business. A fellow named Gordon Plant owns several big trains. He's a comparative newcomer here, I understand. He horned in on the Mexican monopoly. I'm just a mite suspicious of him, but there's no proof that he has been back of the things that have happened. Down in Mexico there are folks who don't look with favor on the coming of the railroad. Wild country down there, with plenty of wild men in it who see a threat to their questionable activities. Then there's old Andy Jorg, who owns

16

a big spread over to the east. His holding includes this section of the desert. He fought me tooth and nail. Refused to sell right-of-way across his land. We had to invoke Eminent Domain to get it. He's mad as Hades and swears he'll wreck the blankety-blank-blank railroad before he's finished with it."

"Sounds like a proddy old gent," Slade commented.

"Uh-huh, he's all of that," Dunn agreed. "Well-heeled, too. Owns a tremendous property. A typical ranch of the Big Bend country, where cows require a vast acreage. A real old-timer, opinionated, stubborn, set in his ways. Has no use for plows, barbed wire, or railroads that come too close. Tried to point out to him that it would be to his advantage to ship from Presidio instead of running his herds north. Couldn't see it. Said his dad and grandad ran their herds all the way to Dodge City, Kansas, and that what was good enough for them was good enough for him."

Slade nodded thoughtfully. He was familiar with the brand —"King Canutes" trying to sweep back the tide of progress with a broom of violence and opposition. Wouldn't work.

"Do you figure Jorg the kind who would resort to such tactics as were employed tonight and the other times you mentioned?" he asked. Dunn shrugged again.

"Frankly, he did not strike me that way," he admitted. "But you never can tell, I've been fooled before. And there's another angle to consider: sometimes a man's workers get out of hand and do things the boss wouldn't countenance." Slade nodded agreement.

"Did you get a good look at those five hellions who threw lead at you?" Dunn asked.

"Only enough to convince me that they were or had been range riders," Slade replied. "I couldn't even say how they were dressed, but the way they sat their horses indicated long familiarity with the saddle. Which, however, has little significance and certainly should not be considered as pointing the finger of suspicion at Jorg." It was Dunn's turn to nod agreement.

"Speaking of cart trains," Slade said, "I've a notion the one I met must have been one of Gordon Plant's trains. I assume he doesn't use Mexicans for carters."

"That's right," answered the G.M. "Texans, I'd say. At least Americans from somewhere in the West."

"And somehow they didn't strike me as the sort really accustomed to following a mule's tail," Slade observed thoughtfully.

17

"Which is something to keep in mind," Dunn remarked sagely.

"Yes, but nothing conclusive about it," Slade pointed out.

"Guess that's so," Dunn conceded. "So we're right back where we started—no proof against anybody. McNelty sent you down here, eh?"

"That's right," Slade replied. "He received your letter and thought it wouldn't do any harm for me to amble down and have a look-see, especially as he didn't have anything else on his mind right then, and was tired of having me hang around the Post."

"Mighty glad you happened to be hanging around handy right at the time," Dunn declared. "I'm feeling better already."

"I hope you won't end up disillusioned," Slade smiled. The General Manager snorted derisively.

"I never have and I don't expect to this time," he said, with emphasis. "Think anybody down here knows you are a Ranger?"

"I doubt it," Slade replied.

"But as El Halcón, yes?"

The devils of laughter in the back of Slade's cold eyes leaped gleefully to the front.

"So I presume," he conceded. Dunn snorted again.

"That fool business of posing as an owlhoot too smart to get caught is going to get you into serious trouble sometime," he predicted gloomily.

"So Captain Jim seems to think, but I'll chance it," Slade answered.

Due to his habit of working undercover whenever possible and often not revealing his Ranger connections, Walt Slade had built up a singular dual reputation. Those who knew the truth declared he was not only the most fearless but also the shrewdest of the Rangers. Others, who did not know the truth and knew him only as El Halcón maintained vigorously that he was just a blasted outlaw who somehow always managed to elude the toils of justice but who would get his comeuppance sooner or later.

Not that all were of that opinion. El Halcón had champions as well as detractors who said, "What if he has got killings to his credit? To his credit is right! Ever hear of him cashing in anybody who didn't have it coming and overdue? That should be left to the duly elected or appointed officers of the law, you say? Uh-huh, but when the duly appointed or elected law officers fall down on the job, it's up to somebody to take over. And that's what El Halcón does. I'm for him!"

And so forth, and so forth, and so forth.

"Well, there's Sam yelpin' for us to come and get it," said the G.M. "He'll have something extra special tonight in your honor; he thinks a lot of you. He's always quoting what the Mexicans say about you—'El Halcón! the friend of the lowly, of all who are wronged or sorrow or are oppressed. El Halcón! the compassionate and the just!' "

"Sam's a fine person," Slade replied, his eyes abruptly all kindness. "I am very fond of him."

"But there's always the chance of some trigger-happy deputy or marshal plugging you by mistake, to say nothing of a gun-slinger out to get a reputation by downing the notorious El Halcón, and not above shooting in the back to get it," Dunn worriedly remarked.

Slade repeated his former careless remark, "I'll chance it. Besides," he added, "there are advantages in being El Halcón. Owlhoots who look on me as one of their own brand are apt to get careless. And as El Halcón there are avenues of information open that would be closed to a known Ranger."

Dunn grunted, and didn't look convinced.

Sam's dinner fulfilled expectations and both railroader and Ranger did it full justice. After which they smoked over final cups of steaming coffee, with little to say, for both were pretty well worn out by strenuous effort and excitement.

Salde slept in the private car and awoke feeling much refreshed and, aside from a slightly sore back, was his normal self again.

"Mistuh Jim is already out on the job," Sam said as he served his breakfast. "He said to let you sleep till you took a notion to wake up."

"That was considerate of him," Slade acknowledged. "I was a mite tuckered, having been in the saddle for about eighteen hours."

"Uh-huh, and on top of that what you went through under that mess," said Sam. "Man, oh man! That was something! You'd oughta been a lot more than a mite tuckered."

Slade enjoyed a leisurely breakfast and after a cigarette and a chat with Sam, he sallied forth in search of Jaggers Dunn.

Everywhere he was greeted by smiles and nods and a waving of hands, the workers regarding him with the greatest respect.

A whisper was running through their ranks—"That's El Halcón, the outlaw!"

"Huh, outlaw or no outlaw, he's the bully boy with a glass

19

eye for my money! If it wasn't for him, Toby would have been a goner. Risked his own life getting under that sill and holding it up with the fire going like blazes over him. Don't let Toby hear you say anything against him; he's liable to take a pick handle to you."

"I was just sayin' what other folks say!"

"The devil with what other folks says! He's okay."

"Right!"

Locating the G.M., Slade found him with a clouded brow and a worried look.

"Things aren't going right at all," he growled. "The men are nervous and jumpy and fumbly. They hesitate to put a pick in the ground for fear of what might happen. Apprehensive about everything they do. And the work is suffering in consequence. Blankety-blank Plant and Jorg!"

Slade nodded without further comment; he was gazing southward, his eyes thoughtful. Dunn regarded him expectantly. He had learned to respect El Halcón's silences, knowing that they usually presaged something important. He was not disappointed in the present instance. Slade abruptly turned to face him.

"A wild country down there," he said, gesturing to the south. "Wild and rugged, but with great potentialities that will be realized with modern transportation. Cattle, wool, wheat, cotton, and other agricultural products. You used wise foresight in planning your line to Chihuahua City."

"So I figured," Dunn replied complacently.

"Of course you know," Slade continued, "that the M.K. Railroad contemplates a line south and west from Del Rio?"

"Of course," Dunn nodded. "Doesn't bother me. They'll be on the other side of the mountains and won't encroach on our territory. No danger of them cutting in on our trade."

"Perhaps," Slade said. "Are you familiar with the country down there, Mr. Dunn?"

"With the survey line, yes," the G.M. replied.

"Ever hear of the Cienaga Pass?" Slade asked.

"Why, no," Dunn answered.

"The same applies to most people up here, and to the majority south of the Rio Grande, for it is not really a pass at all, being unapproachable from the east for horses or carts. It's a canyon that runs right through the mountains, from east to west. As I said, it cannot be negotiated from the east, for it boxes on the east by perpendicular cliffs, not very high but unclimbable."

"Then what good is the darn thing?" Dunn asked, although

20

Slade was convinced that his quick mind had already grasped the implication.

"For nothing as is," Slade replied. "But with modern excavation methods it would be no great chore to dig and blast an opening on the east. Then you'd have an almost water-level route through the mountains, not far south of the Rio Grande, and a straight shoot to tap the territory you hope to exploit."

"And you think—" Dunn began, his eyes snapping.

"I rather more than think," Slade answered. "As it happened, last year, before you revealed your intention of a line to Presidio and on to Chihuahua City, I was trailing a certain gent I thought used the canyon for a shortcut. I was mistaken in that, as I realized when I came up against the box end of the canyon. But," he added impressively, "while I was in there, I saw stakes and other unmistakeable evidence that a survey line had been run through the canyon. Right then I was at a loss to comprehend what it meant. Wasn't much interested, anyhow. Had other matters in urgent need of attention. But when I heard you had started this line and received the letter you wrote Captain Jim, I began to get an inkling of what it might mean, having already heard of the M.K. plans to build south and west from Del Rio. So you see it may not be either Jorg or Plant who is responsible for your troubles. You are familiar with the M.K. methods and know that ethics is just a word they may have noted in the dictionary. Beginning to get the notion?"

Dunn swore with explosive violence. "You're blasted well right I am," he growled.

"So," Slade concluded, "you may have something in the nature of a railroad building race on your hands. The first to get through to Chihuahua will be in a position to negotiate mail, express and shipping contracts. Delaying tactics may well be in order, something you have encountered before."

"Uh-huh, and a couple of times you pulled the fat out of the fire for me," Dunn said. "Now you've really got me bothered, for I never knew anybody who could sum up a situation faster or more accurately. I'm afraid you're right this time, too. Confound it! I can't fight fire with fire. I'm just not made that way."

Slade nodded sober agreement. Jim Dunn was a square-shooter and would never stoop to unethical practices no matter how great the provocation.

"You going to stick around?" Dunn asked.

"That's what I'm here for, is it not?" Slade countered. "I

21

was sent here to investigate your complaint of unlawful activities going on in this section. Last night was an example of sabotage that might well have cost one or more lives. As a Texas Ranger that is very much my business, and it is my duty to see, if possible, that the culprits are brought to justice.

"They'll be brought to justice, all right," Dunn predicted grimly, "but as to whether they'll ever stand trial is problematical. I've noticed that in such cases, El Halcón is quite often judge, jury, prosecutor and executioner. Well, often that's the only way to do it, so more power to you. Now I suppose you'll need an excuse to stick around, so how about taking charge of things here? After all, I have a few more things to think about other than this blasted feeder; I've been away from the main office too long as it is. Although you're not working at it, I don't believe there's a better engineer in Texas, and you have a rare knack, something born to, not acquired, for inspiring men to be fiercely loyal to you. Already the boys admire and respect you for what you did last night, and I'm confident you won't have any trouble with them."

"Thank you for your confidence in me, sir," Slade replied. "But don't you have a field engineer on this job?"

"Yes, I have," Dunn replied. "John Butler, a first rate construction man, but I'm afraid he doesn't get the work out of the boys he should. He's down at Presidio right now, superintending the construction of the approaches for the bridge across the Rio Grande, a highly important project as you well know."

"Decidedly so," Slade conceded. "Did Butler run the surveys for the approaches?" Dunn shook his head.

"There's another example of the bad luck that"s been dogging me ever since I conceived this project," he said. "The surveys were run by Potter Quigley, a good bridge engineer, but right after he finished that part of the chore he took sick and quit. Said the climate down here would kill him if he stayed. Could be; it is a devil of a section for anybody not accustomed to such conditions. I was planning to try and transfer another man here, later, although it would disrupt other work to do so. Now with you here I don't have to worry about that, if you'll take over."

"Perhaps Mr. Butler won't take kindly to being superceded, which is what it amounts to," Slade suggested. Dunn chuckled.

"Well," he said dryly, "having seen you in action a few times, I predict that if his dissatisfaction proves too vocal he is liable all of a sudden to wonder how come the sky fell in on him."

Slade laughed. "I've a notion Mr. Butler and I will make out together," he replied. "Yes, I'll take over the chore—gives me a chance to keep my hand in, as it were."

"Still planning to go in for engineering?" Dunn asked curiously.

"Oh, sure," Slade admitted. "After a while, when I decide to leave the Rangers." Dunn smiled and did not comment.

"Come on over to the car and I'll give you your authority," he said.

FOUR

IN THE PRIVATE CAR the General Manager scratched away busily with a pen for a few minutes. He read over what he had written, affixed his signature, and handed the paper to Slade, who glanced at it, folded it and stowed it in a pocket.

"That should hold you," Dunn said cheerfully.

"Yes," Slade smiled, "even to cleaning out the office safe if I take a notion to."

"Go to it!" Dunn replied blithely. "If you do, I've a notion you will have earned it. Now what?"

"Now," Slade said, "I think I'll ride down to Presidio to see what you're trying to put over on 'Ol' Debbil River.' Never bridged the Rio Grande, have you?"

"No," Dunn admitted, "but with your help I bridged the Pecos, if you'll recall."

"Yes," Slade nodded. "But compared to the Rio Grande when it takes a notion to really go on a rampage, the Pecos is like a purry kitten to a catamount."

"Okay," said Dunn. "You have authority to change the course of the river if you decide it expedient to do so."

"The Rio Grande takes care of that angle without any outside help," Slade answered. "That's one of the problems with which you'll have to contend. One slip in planning those approaches and you'll find yourself without a bridge."

"I have had such a notion," Dunn admitted. "However, Quigley seemed to be a capable man and doubtless you'll find everything okay. Anyhow, with you on the job I figure my troubles there are over. Be seeing you when you get back."

Jaggers Dunn was right when he observed that Walt Slade was an engineer and a good one. Shortly before the death of his father, which followed financial reverses that entailed the loss of the elder Slade's ranch, young Walt had graduated from a famous college of engineering. His intention had been to take a post-graduate course in special subjects to round out his education and better fit him for the profession he had determined to make his life work. That, however, became impossible for the time being and Slade was undecided as to just what to do. He had about made up his mind to accept a position with an engineering firm when he happened to drop in on Captain Jim McNelty, the famous

24

Commander of the Border Battalion of the Texas Rangers. Captain Jim had a suggestion to make.

"Walt," he said, "why don't you come into the Rangers for a while? You liked the chore when you worked with me some during summer vacations. It would give you plenty of spare time for study and keep you going comfortably at the same time."

After due consideration, Slade concluded the notion was a good one. He signed up with the Rangers. Long since he had obtained more from private study than he could have hoped for from the post-grad and was eminently fitted to take up the profession of engineering.

Meanwhile, however, Ranger work had gotten a strong hold on him, providing as it did so many opportunities for helping his fellow men and making the world a better place for decent people to live. So he hesitated to sever connections with the illustrious body of law enforcement officers. Plenty of time to be an engineer—he was young. Eventually he would become one, but not just yet. He would stick with the Rangers for a while.

After leaving Jaggers Dunn, Slade got the rig on Shadow and rode south at a fair pace. Gradually the desert became less austere and the going more comfortable. Eventually, without incident, he sighted Presidio, an old town of sun-baked houses squatting in the shade of giant cottonwoods. It had a leisurely look, but he knew it could be plenty rambunctious at times, and was. The same went for Ojinaga, the Mexican town across the river. Presidio was and still is a minor port of entry into Mexico. It was here that the Chihuahua Trail, one of the main freight routes into Mexico, crossed the Rio Grande, The miners and ranchers of the surrounding mountains obtain supplies at Presidio and would welcome the railroad shipping facilities. They also found diversion in the saloons and cantinas of Presidio and Ojinaga and livened things by their presence. Now the railroad construction workers were adding their bit to the general hilarity.

Several hundred yards beyond the outskirts of the town, a large crew of workmen were busily preparing the northern approach to the contemplated bridge. Slade rode to the scene of operations and studied the site. His lips pursed in a soundless whistle.

Directing the activities of the workers was a big, burly man with a bad-tempered face. Slade dismounted and approached him.

"Mr. Butler, is it not?" El Halcón asked, as the big man turned questioningly.

"That's right," the other rumbled. Slade supplied his own name and they shook hands, Butler looking even more questioning. He had a grip and evidently liked to use it, but when their hands fell apart there were white circles around his fingers. He shot Slade a look of grudging respect but did not comment. Doubtless desiring to change the subject, he gestured to the work.

"Well, cowboy, what do you think of it?" he asked.

"I think," Slade replied quietly, "that some changes will have to be made." Butler stared.

"What!" he exclaimed.

"Mr. Butler," Slade said, "are you acquainted with the vagaries of this river?"

"Never laid eyes on the blasted thing till I came down here to take charge," Butler replied. "Why? And what do you mean about changes being made?"

"I mean," Slade said, "that the approach must be placed above the bend in the river, not below it. Here you will very likely, sooner or later, find your approach under ten feet of water that will gnaw out the foundations of your pier."

The big fellow bristled. "Say!" he demanded truculently, "who the devil are you to come here and try to tell me my business?"

In answer, Slade slipped the folded paper from his pocket and handed it to him. The astounded engineer read, in a handwriting like a barbed wire railing and over the indubitable signature of General Manager James G. Dunn—"To all officers and employees of the C. &. P. Railroad System: orders issued by the bearer, Walter J. Slade, are to be obeyed at once, without question, and to the letter."

Butler looked dazed. "Does this mean the Old Man is firing me?" he asked.

"Certainly not," Slade assured him. "Mr. Dunn has every confidence in your ability as a construction man, but I understand you are not a bridge engineer."

"That's right," Butler admitted, "but Mr. Quigley, who laid out the survey for this approach, is a good one."

"Perhaps," Slade conceded, "but not a good geologist. Otherwise he would have seen that the river has been here before. You said you are not conversant with the vagaries of the Rio Grande. It is a most unpredictable stream and changes its bed without warning. A man living in Texas today may find himself living in Mexico tomorrow morning. Something that must be taken into consideration when a

26

bridge is contemplated. I presume that Mr. Quigley was also not familiar with the river, although his branch of the profession entails a certain geologic knowledge. Somehow he slipped there. The survey of the approach is excellent; he evidently knows that branch of his business. But the angle of crossing is wrong. It must be a thirty-degree angle from downstream to the Mexican shore. And I want the piers anchored to bedrock."

"Mr. Quigley felt the parent clay would be sufficient," Butler interpolated.

"It wouldn't be," Slade differed shortly. "Anchor on bedrock. Now I'll show you where to plan your Texas approach. Come along."

With Shadow pacing sedately behind, they walked upstream until they were not far from the outskirts of the town. Slade paused and gazed across the now placid stream.

"Here is where you will begin your survey," he said. "The pier a hundred feet from the low water mark. How does Quigley's survey compare with that?"

"He estimated fifty feet," Butler replied. "Said the closer to the water the less steel required, and steel costs money."

"Too much to risk a bridge full of it resting on the bottom of the Rio Grande," Slade said. "A hundred feet from the low water mark. Got that clear?"

Butler drew forth a notebook and jotted down figures. "All set, sir," he said. "Now what?"

"You feel you are competent to make the survey? I presume you are. If not, I will take care of it."

"Yes, I can make the survey," Butler replied. For the first time a smile brightened his bad-tempered countenance.

"Nice to have somebody take over some of the responsibility," he said. "And now?"

"Now," Slade repeated, "I'd like to have you get the men together; I have a few words to say to them."

They walked back to the scene of operations. Butler let out a few shouts and soon had the workers assembled before them, looking expectant.

"Men," said Butler, "this is Mr. Slade, the new Big Boss; he has something to say to you."

Slade swept the group with his cold eyes; he sensed a certain resentment, a touch of apprehension. Suddenly he smiled, the flashing white smile of El Halcón which men, and women, find irresistible. In a moment there were answering grins, a change of attitude. His deep musical voice rang out—

"Fellows, I understood from Mr. Dunn that a date has

27

been set for the completion of this project, and that Mr. Dunn is very anxious that it be completed by that date. Okay. For every day less than the number of days specified, there will be a bonus of a full day's pay at overtime rates. So if you're looking forward to a really big bust when the chore is finished, go to it!"

For a moment there was a surprised silence, then a voice shouted—

"Hurrah for the Old Man!" The cheer was given with a will.

"Knock off for the day," Slade said, smiling broadly. He knew that the title "Old Man," no matter what the recipient's years, was the highest accolade these rough and ready workers could accord a boss. Another cheer followed and the workers headed for Presidio and a mite of celebration.

"You've got 'em, sir," chuckled Butler. "They'll spit in the Devil's eyes for you from now on."

"No sense in them wasting their time here," Slade said. "It will take you a day at least to complete your survey and line up the project, so let them take it easy till you're ready for them. Now supposed you and I amble up to Presidio and have a snort and something to eat."

"Suits me," agreed Butler. "I know a place where they put out good chuck. Likker ain't bad, either, and the games are straight and the girls—accommodating."

"Sounds interesting," Slade answered.

"Called the Churn Head, from a horse, I reckon," said Butler. "Feller named Pickle Simon runs it. Where he got his moniker I *don't* know. Sort of reminds me of a Mother Goose rhyme."

"And speaking of horses," Slade observed, "I'll need a place where my cayuse can put on the nosebag and sleep comfortable."

"I'll show you to Amado's stable, I keep my horse there," Butler offered. "He's a Mexican and a good *amigo*."

"Fine," Slade replied. "Mexicans usually run good stables. The majority of them have a way with horses and horses take to them."

"That's been my experience," Butler nodded. "Some folks don't like Mexicans, but I've found 'em just the same as other people—mostly good, with now and then a bad one, like everywhere and everybody."

"You're right, there," Slade agreed. He was beginning to like John Butler who, truculent and apt to fly off the handle, nevertheless impressed him as being honest and with good principles. He decided to have a little confidential chat with the engineer, later.

FIVE

AT THE LIVERY STABLE, a smiling old Mexican was properly introduced to Shadow, after bowing low to Slade who greeted him in flawless Spanish, to the old fellow's unconcealed delight. Butler evidently noticed the respect accorded his companion but said nothing.

"And now *we'll* put on the nosebag," he announced. "I figure it's been a good day and feel like putting away a hefty surrounding."

Slade slanted him a sideways glance. "Brought up on the range, were you not, Mr. Butler?" he remarked.

"That's right," the engineer replied. "Started out following a cow's tail, as I've a notion you did, too. Worked my way through school and college and got my degree. I've still got a lot to learn, but I hope to get there and be a topflight engineer."

"And I have not the slightest doubt but that you'll do it," Slade said, and meant it.

"Yes, a topflight engineer, like yourself," Butler said, adding a little wistfully, "but I fear I lack something that you have."

"Yes? What's that?" Slade prompted.

"The ability," Butler replied slowly, "to have men follow you wherever you choose to lead, no matter how tough the going or how lopsided the odds. With just a few words today you cemented the loyalty of those roughnecks. No matter what you propose, you won't have to look back to see if they're coming along. If you take a notion to lead an expedition into Mexico and capture Chihuahua City, they'll be right there in the front rank with you."

Slade laughed heartily. "I don't think they'll be required to make such a sacrifice," he chuckled. "But thank you for saying it. Well, this looks like your Churn Head saloon. At least that's what the name on the window says."

"Yep, this is it," said Butler. "In we go."

The Churn Head was big, well lighted, and busy, a typical border town saloon. There was a long bar, already fairly well crowded although it was still early in the evening, a dance floor, a couple of roulette wheels, a faro bank, poker tables, a lunch counter, and tables for more leisurely diners.

"Here comes Pickle," said Butler as they sat down at a

29

table which Slade chose because, although Butler didn't know it, it afforded a clear view of the swinging doors, an act habitual with El Halcón.

Pickle Simon, big, lanky, spindle-legged, and long-armed, had the lugubrious expression of a well-vinegared pickle, which was perhaps the derivative of his unusual nickname, but there were grin quirkings at the corners of his mouth and a twinkle in the depths of his deep-set blue eyes. Altogether, he reminded Slade of a rather mournful stork.

"Howdy, Mr. Butler, it's sure a nice day," he said sadly. "Glad to have you with us." He glanced suggestively at Slade. Butler performed the introductions and Pickle shook hands with a good grip.

"How be *you?*" he said dolefully. "I'll send over a drink."

"He's all right, even though he does talk as if somebody'd swiped the silver lining of his cloud," chuckled Butler.

"From Down East, eh?" Slade remarked.

"Believe somebody did say he comes from Vermont," agreed Butler. "How'd you guess it?"

"Very seldom that you hear the expression, 'be you' other than in New England," Slade explained.

"Don't miss much, do you?" Butler said admiringly. "Here come the snorts, and I figure I can use one. To bridges that won't wash away!"

Slade smiled, and drank the toast with him. Despite his evident somewhat irascible disposition, John Butler had a sense of humor.

Their meal arrived and they set to with appetite. While they were eating, the orchestra filed in, the dance-floor girls put in an appearance and soon the evening's entertainment was in full swing. For it was now full dark and the Churn Head was becoming crowded.

Butler suddenly uttered an exclamation. Slade glanced at him inquiringly.

"That's old Andy Jorg, who owns the Barred Diamond ranch. Just came in with some of his hands." Butler explained. "He hasn't any use for the railroad."

Slade had already noted the slender, neatly dressed elderly man who had just entered with half a dozen cowhands trailing after him. He had a handsome, though lined face, quick, alert gray eyes and a tight mouth. His movements were graceful and assured. But Slade seemed to sense an aura of loneliness that enveloped him, the loneliness of a man who has everything but still has nothing. He wondered just what was the old fellow's history; would very likely be interesting to read.

30

Jorg's gaze swept the room, centered for an instant on the table occupied by Slade and Butler, then shifted aside.

"The big fellow beside him is Hal Murdock, his range boss," Butler remarked. "A hard character and a tough man in a rough-and-tumble I understand."

Slade studied Murdock a moment and decided that Butler very likely had sized him up correctly. He was a giant of a man, approaching middle age, with thick and slightly bowed shoulders, long, dangling arms and blunt-fingered hands. His clear brown eyes shot glances in every direction as he shouldered his way to the bar, making room for Jorg. Slade noted that the Barred Diamond bunch were close to a group of the railroad construction men, numbering seven or eight.

Jorg and his men ordered drinks and stood talking together, apparently paying no attention to the other occupants of the bar. Slade turned back to Butler.

"I gathered from Mr. Dunn that you do not anticipate any trouble with the steel work of the bridge," he observed. Butler shook his head vigorously.

"Steel is steel and I've had plenty of experience with it," he replied. "Besides, I have a couple of good foremen who know all the angles of steel. With the approaches and piers where they should be, as they will be now, I'll go along skalleyhooting. Approaches and piers are something with which I've had no experience. That's why Mr. Dunn sent Quigley to handle that angle."

"I see," Slade said thoughtfully. "Tomorrow I'll head back for the camp and start the wagons rolling down here with the stone for the piers. I noticed several carloads already on a siding up there."

"Fine!" exclaimed Butler. "With the boys bending their backs like they'll be doing for you, we'll be ready for it soon. Say! looks like an argument starting at the bar."

Slade nodded. Watching the two groups, he had seen that they were throwing remarks back and forth, voices loudening.

Somebody went too far. A fist swung. Instantly that whole end of the bar was a kicking, clawing, hitting tussle.

Butler started to rise, but Slade, rather amused by the ruckus typical of men who knew little of the manly art of self defense, laid a restraining hand on his arm.

"Let them alone," he advised. "It's just a fist wring with no real harm in it. Pickle and his floor men will break it up in a minute."

As might have been expected, Hal Murdock, the big range boss, was in the forefront of the row. Old Andy Jorg, standing

31

a little back, viewed the disturbance with a cynical smile.

Abruptly things got serious. Murdock caught a good one that sent him reeling. He bawled an oath, jerked his gun and flung it high for a lethal blow with the heavy barrel.

Walt Slade's hand moved like a blur of light. The hanging lamps jumped to the crash of a shot.

Hal Murdock gave a yelp of pain. His gun, the lock smashed by Slade's bullet, thudded to the floor half a dozen yards distant.

The two groups fell apart, staring at Slade, who holstered his still smoking Colt and strode across to confront Murdock.

"What's the matter with you, fellow?" he asked. "Can't you have a sociable wring without trying to kill somebody?"

Murdock, rubbing his tingling hand, glared at him. "I'll wring *you!*" he howled and launched a blow at Slade's face.

Before it traveled six inches it was blocked and a sizzling left hook purpled Murdock's cheekbone. He swayed back, tripped over his own feet and hit the floor with a crash. Mouthing curses, he scrambled erect and rushed, and caught another hook that sent him off balance for an instant.

Slade did not follow up his advantage but waited for Murdock to recover. He was not particularly worried about the outcome although he knew he had a fight on his hands. Murdock outweighed him by perhaps thirty pounds, he was quick on his feet and he could hit. In he came again, got past Slade's guard and rocked his head with an uppercut, followed by a solid smash to the chest that caused the Ranger to give ground. Murdock made the mistake of coming in too fast and caught another stinging hook, this time to the nose, that sent blood spurting from that member. And Slade decided it was time to stop fooling with him. He had noted that Murdock was left-handed, that he hit mostly with his right. But in his passive left, Slade felt the real threat lay. He weaved aside as Murdock rushed again, stepped on a wet cigar butt that slid under his foot and floundered for an instant. Murdock bounded in for the kill, and over came the left.

But with cat-like agility, Slade recovered, jerked his head aside and the big fist whizzed over his shoulder. His own hand shot forward in a straight right with all his two hundred muscular pounds behind it, catching Murdock squarely on the angle of the jaw and lifting him clean off his feet. He hit the floor with a crash and that time he stayed there,

32

gulping and groaning and rolling his bristly red head from side to side.

Slade slanted a glance at the Barred Diamond bunch. They were standing rigid, not moving a hand.

Not surprising, however. Pickle Simon was regarding them dejectedly over the twin muzzles of a cocked, sawed-off shot-gun.

"Guess that'll be about all, gents," he said lugubriously. "Somebody help Murdock to stand up."

It was Slade who helped the range boss to rise. Murdock, rubbing his swelling jaw gazed at him a moment. Then the fire in his deep-set eyes softened to a sly and humorous twinkle.

"Feller, you're good, darned good," he said, still working on the jaw. "Ain't been hit so hard since I told my dad I was too big to whup and he showed me I wasn't, with a scantlin'. Hope there's no hard feelings; I sure don't hold any, and here's my hand on it."

He thrust forth his big paw as he spoke and they shook solemnly, smiling into each other's eyes. Slade felt it would not be hard to like Hal Murdock. He turned at a touch on his elbow to face old Andy Jorg's cold stare.

"So!" Jorg said softly. "So Dunn has brought in a professional gun-slinger and fancy man to do his fighting for him."

"Not necessarily to do fighting, but if any is brought my way I aim to accommodate," Slade replied.

For a moment their glances locked like rapier blades. Jorg's eyes were first to slide away. He turned to his men.

"Come on, let's get out of here," he said. The hands dutifully obeyed. Hal Murdock, who evidently wasn't afraid of his boss, picked up his battered gun and winked at Slade as they passed through the swinging doors. Slade went back to his table where Butler had already resumed his seat.

"You're good with your hands, Mr. Slade, mighty good," the engineer said. "But when it comes to shooting—Gentl-l-lmen hush! I never saw anything like it. In fact I didn't really see at all. It just happened."

Slade smiled deprecatingly. "I was lucky and didn't miss," he replied. "I feared that with his weight back of the blow, he might have seriously injured someone, and figured I'd better try and stop him."

"You stopped him, all right, in various ways," Butler agreed dryly. "And he's a tough customer."

"I figure he's all right, but with a loosely *látigoed* temper," Slade commented.

Butler nodded dubiously, apparently not precisely agreeing with Slade's estimate of Hal Murdock.

"What do you think of old Jorg?" he asked.

"A dangerous man," Slade replied briefly.

"Yes?"

"Yes. He has what Murdock does not, perfect control of his emotions and a cool, calculating brain. Andy Jorg can be somebody to reckon with."

"My sentiments," said Butler. "Do you figure it's him that's been causing the trouble for the road?"

"Frankly, I don't know," Slade replied. "He doesn't look like that sort, but I could be mistaken. When a man really gets his bristles up over something, it is sometimes surprising the lengths to which he will go. Could be the case with Jorg who is an old-timer and bitterly resentful of anything that threatens the existing order, which he firmly believes is just as it should be and cannot be bettered. None are so blind as those who will not see. Jorg may have to be enlightened, perhaps in the manner in which Pharaoh was enlightened, by sorrow and tribulation." Butler nodded sober agreement.

"By the way," Slade said, "do you know anything much about Potter Quigley, the bridge engineer who quit on account of ill health?"

"Why, not a great deal," Butler answered. "I understand he came to the C. & P. from the Weston people who recommended him highly."

"A competent and trustworthy firm," Slade commented. "Do you know whom he was with before joining the Weston Company?"

"No, I don't," Butler replied. "I don't recall him ever mentioning it."

John Butler was not slow-witted and he regarded Slade curiously for a moment.

"Mr. Slade," he said, "just what is back of those questions? You must have a reason for asking them."

"Mr. Butler, I have," Slade admitted. "As you must know—"

The grin that so changed Butler's expression suddenly flashed out.

"Say!" he interrupted, "don't you think we can do away with the Mistering? Looks like we'll be associated for quite some time, so why not drop the formality?"

"Okay, John," Slade smiled. "As you must know, a competent bridge engineer such as Potter Quigley appears to be would undoubtedly realize that those approaches and the

34

sites for the piers are wrong. Does it seem reasonable that Quigley should make such a glaring error?"

Butler stroked his stubborn chin a moment before replying.

"Walt, it doesn't," he said. "I've been wondering about it ever since you showed me the error."

"So perhaps you'll understand the reason for my questions," Slade said. "I'd certainly like to learn something relative to Potter Quigley's background, and I intend to try. At present the evidence points not to a miscalculation but a deliberate attempt to put in a bridge that sooner or later the Rio Grande would destroy. Quite likely sooner, for fast approaching is the season of violent storms on the upper river and its tributaries. If the Rio Grande suddenly comes down in flood we'll have trouble enough on our hands without a shaky bridge to worry about. As I said, the Rio Grande is a most unpredictable stream and it's wise to expect the worst."

"But why should Quigley do such a thing—what has he to gain by it?" Butler wanted to know.

"At the present, your guess is as good as mine," Slade replied. He did not care to mention his suspicion that probably the M. &. K. Railroad, the C. & P.'s great rival, had something to do with the business, for all he had to go on *was* suspicion.

"I wonder," Butler remarked reflectively, "if Gordon Plant, who owns the carting lines, could be back of what happened?"

"I will have to hold judgment on Plant in abeyance until I meet him and learn more about him," Slade answered. "Plant might gain a temporary pecuniary advantage by delaying the road, but certainly not enough to warrant risking a penitentiary sentence or the noosed end of a rope if somebody happened to be killed in the course of such depredations. Unless he is absolutely terrapin-brained he must know that he can't hope to stop the railroad. But, as I said, men do strange things in a moment of anger or resentment, so we can't altogether rule out Gordon Plant."

"Guess you're right," agreed Butler. "How do you feel? You took a couple of hot ones during your shindig with Murdock."

"My ribs are a mite sore, and so is my jaw, but nothing to really bother about," Slade answered. "The big jigger can hit, but nothing like he would be able to if he learned to really use his strength. And to control his temper, which is his great weakness. In his anger he laid himself wide open."

"Uh-huh, to somebody who knows how to take advantage of it," Butler grunted. "I sure wouldn't want to tangle with him, and he ain't so much bigger than me, either. The way you handled him was something!"

"I'll stay with you tomorrow until you get your survey started," Slade deftly changed the subject. "Then I'll ride back to the camp for a talk with Mr. Dunn before he leaves for Chicago, which he wishes to do as soon as possible. Also, I hope to speed up the work on the iron; the quicker we get the tracks laid to here the better. Freighting material by wagon is expensive and slow. And very soon you'll be needing plenty of steel, which isn't easy to transport by wagon."

Pickle Simon, the owner, strolled over to the table. "Much obliged, Mr. Slade, for keeping something really bad from happening," he said. "Was almighty funny, the way you larruped Hal Murdock. Cussed if I didn't come nigh to laughing out loud when he walked into that last one," he added sadly. "Hal's all right but a mite uppity and holds his comb a bit too high. He needed to be taken down a peg."

"I don't think he was much affected one way or another," Slade returned. "I've a notion he really likes fighting."

"Could be," conceded Pickle. "Well, you sure got all the boys talking and all the girls looking. Hope you'll come back, Mr. Slade. Usually sorta peaceful and homey here. I'll send over a drink."

After they finished the drink, Slade said, "Now I think I'll go to bed. Getting late and I want to be up early tomorrow."

"Me, too," replied Butler. "I'll get busy on the surveys first thing in the morning. I sleep in a hotel here in town—the boys sleep at the camp. You can get a room, I'm pretty sure. Okay?"

"That'll be fine," Slade said. "All set? Let's go."

At the bar, a burly railroader accosted Slade. "Much obliged, sir, for saving me a split noggin," he said. "I thought I was a goner when Murdock pulled that gun."

"Glad to have been able to help," Slade replied, and shook the hand the worker diffidently extended.

As he and Butler passed through the swinging doors, they heard a voice say proudly to a new arrival, "That's our Old Man, a right *hombre*."

SIX

IN A COMFORTABLE BED, Slade slept soundly till morning. After breakfast he repaired to the scene of operations near the river bank. There he found Butler and his crews already busily at work. Shouts and a waving of hands greeted his appearance. He smiled and waved back to the workers and approached the engineer.

"Everything going along fine," said Butler; "the boys sure are bending their backs. They'll make up the lost time before you know it. But I hope you'll be here to help me line up the middle pier in the river; I feel sorta shaky about that."

"Yes, I'll be here," Slade promised. "Don't worry, there won't be any trouble. Now I'm heading back to the main camp for a conflab with Mr. Dunn. He'll be pleased to learn how expertly you're handling things here. As I said in the beginning, he has faith in your ability and will be glad to have his judgment vindicated."

Butler looked very pleased. "Much obliged again for everything," he said. "Be seeing you." He hurried back to his work. Slade watched a few minutes then headed for the stable to get the rig on Shadow. He found the big black in first class condition and rarin' to go.

However, Slade did not head directly for the main construction camp. Instead, he followed the course of the river, which here ran almost due north with a trending to the west, for a mile or so above the town. Finally he pulled to a halt and sat studying the stream, not altogether with satisfaction.

He was at the apex of a second bend, sharper than the one below Presidio. The bank was high and steep, but where he sat his horse was actually below the high water mark. A break-through here would do a nice job of flooding. The results would not be so disastrous as a break-through at the bend below the town, but would cause plenty of trouble and delay. He put the possibility in the back of his mind for further consideration and turned Shadow's nose toward the railhead construction camp.

Aside from the discomfort of the blistering heat and its reflection upward from the sands, he suffered no inconvenience in the course of the ride. Arriving at the railhead, which was now nearly a mile below the camp site, he found Jaggers Dunn directing things, as usual. The G.M. waved a hand and glanced at him expectantly as Slade reined in beside him.

"I'd like to have a talk with you, sir, at your earliest convenience," he said. A single look told the General Manager that something was in the wind.

"Okay," he said, "put up your critter and I'll be right with you soon as I make sure of the set of these blasted fish plates. Some of 'em are a mite off size, but I'll be hanged if I know why. They should all be standard. Seems everything goes haywire of late."

Slade rode on and cared for Shadow. In the private car, Sam brought him a cup of coffee and he relaxed comfortably with a cigarette to await the appearance of the sturdy old empire builder who would scorn transportation and trudge all the way in the broiling sun.

In a surprisingly short time, Dunn arrived, fanning his perspiring face with his hat. Sam hurried to bring him coffee, too.

"Nothing like hot coffee on a hot day," Jaggers declared, taking a swig. "Cold drinks just make you hotter. Okay, what you got on your mind? Trouble, I bet."

"I'm afraid so, although I think by now it's well on the way to being remedied," Slade replied. "Here's how the situation did stand, and how it stands now."

With which he launched into an account of what he found on the banks of the Rio Grande. Jaggers Dunn listened attentively, then did some very creditable swearing.

"And you figure the blankety-blank-blank deliberately planned to have the bridge go out with the first flood or break-through?"

"Well, it looks that way to me," Slade conceded. "I can't see a man of Quigley's undoubted ability making such a colossal blunder. Can you?"

"No, I can't," growled Dunn. "Thank Pete you happened along when you did. I figured I wouldn't be needed down there for a while and by now, if you hadn't showed up, the chances are I'd have been on my way to Chicago thinking everything was under control. And now what?"

"And now," Slade replied, glancing at the telegraph instrument on a nearby table, "now try and learn from the Weston people what was Quigley's background before he came to them, whom he worked for prior to his employment with the Weston firm. They should have all the data. I can't see them hiring a man for a responsible position such as Quigley must have held without investigating his recommendations."

38

"Right you are," agreed Dunn. "I know Archibald Worthington, the president of the Weston Company, know him well. Arch will get everything there is to learn about the scalawag. I'll start the wire humming right now. If I get through to Arch without delay, we should have a return wire from him before nightfall."

He moved to the instrument and began clicking out a lengthy message. Slade relaxed comfortably in his chair and rolled another cigarette, his mind at ease. For he knew that there would be no delay in the transmission; when Jaggers Dunn spoke, either by voice or telegraph, folks jumped.

After a bit, Dunn closed the key and resumed his chair and coffee cup.

"That should do it," he said. "Anything else happen while you were down there?"

Slade regaled him with an account of the row in the saloon. Dunn stroked his crinkly white mane with a big hand and looked thoughtful.

"Hmmm!" he commented. "So you got a look at Andy Jorg, eh? What do you think of him?"

"I'm not prepared to express a positive opinion just yet," Slade replied. "A hard man, all right, arrogant, self-centered, accustomed to having his own way, hates to be crossed. As to just how far he might be inclined to go in a moment of anger, I'd prefer not to hazard a guess at present. Only somehow I can't help but feel that his methods would be direct. As to that, though, I also would prefer not to be dogmatic. Easy to make a mistake where such an individaul is concerned."

Dunn nodded thoughtfully and helped himself to a cigar. For some time they smoked in silence, until Sam called from the dining compartment,

"Lunch on the table, boss men."

They enjoyed a leisurely meal, then relaxed a while, discussing various matters. Finally, Dunn said, "Let's go outside and look around a bit. Time to introduce you to the boys. Not that they don't all know you already; they're still talking about what you did the other night."

The workers were streaming out of the dining cars, having just finished their noonday meal. Dunn beckoned one, who came forward.

"Slade, this is Casey, the head foreman," Dunn said. "Casey, Mr. Slade will be in charge here from now on. I expect any orders he issues to be obeyed without question."

39

Casey, lean, wizened, with bright beady eyes, writhed his thin lips in a chuckle.

"Well, sir, I don't think anybody will do any questioning," he replied. "Not after seeing Mr. Slade lift a boxcar with his back the other night. The boys are a fine healthy lot and they hanker to stay healthy."

"Okay," Jaggers nodded. "And, Casey, get an engine hooked to my car; I'm heading for the mainline soon, I hope. Well, Walt, I guess that takes care of everything; you're on your own from now on. I've got a lot of paper work to do, and I'll be rolling as soon as we get a reply from the Weston people, which should be any hour, now. I'll send for you when it arrives."

He strode back to the car, with a springy step a man twenty years younger might well envy. Slade turned to Casey.

"Call the boys together," he directed. Casey did so and soon a dense crowd of uplifted faces were regarding him expectantly.

"Fellows," he said, "I want the work to progress, but I don't want any rushing or hurrying, not in this heat. The desert can be deadly, and it'll get worse day by day as the sun moves farther north. Another six or seven miles and things will be better. You are experienced track men and know that a steady and easy pace pays off in the end. That's all for the time being. I'm depending on you."

A cheer went up, then the workers trooped off to their chores. Casey repeated John Butler's words, "You've got 'em, sir. Yes, you've got the terriers and you don't have to worry about the work not going ahead as it should."

"I hope so," Slade replied. He glanced around.

"Later in the afternoon, hook an engine onto those cars of stone for the bridge piers and run them out onto the mainline," he directed. "First thing in the morning we'll roll them down to the railhead, where the wagons will be ready to load them and take off for the Rio Grande."

"Certain," replied Casey. "I'll see to it, Mr. Slade."

Accompanied by Casey, Slade inspected the work. Here where the terrain was favorable, several sidings had already been laid and several more were in course of construction. Their purpose to relieve the pressure on the contemplated assembly yard at Presidio.

"They'll be needed," Slade said. "The line is going to carry a tremendous freightage to and from Mexico once it gets going good. Mr. Dunn is a man of foresight and realizes that."

40

"He's okay," said Casey. "I've been with him for fifteen years and better and I know."

The afternoon was well along when a man came hurrying up to Slade.

"Mr. Dunn would like to see you in his car," he told the Ranger.

In the private car, Slade found Jaggers Dunn sitting at his desk and staring at words written on a sheet of paper.

"Got a reply from Arch Worthington of the Weston people," he announced. "Quite a dossier on Potter Quigley. He came to them from the R. I. & J. Before that he was with the L. H. & V. Before that the Great Eastern. First rate recommendations all the way. What do you think of that?"

"Looks like we're sort of left hanging in the air," Slade answered. "In my opinion, none of those roads ever had any connections with the M.K."

"That's right," nodded Dunn.

"So it would appear that my theory that Quigley might have been planted with the C. & P. by the M.K. people falls to the ground," Slade said.

"Yes, looks a little that way," Dunn agreed. He paused for a moment.

"I wonder if Quigley might have made an honest mistake," he added slowly.

"Anything is possible," Slade answered, without committing himself further.

"But you don't think so," Dunn shot at him.

"No, I don't."

"I see," Dunn said, and paused again. "Begins to look a little like Andy Jorg is our man, after all," he resumed. "As I told you before, he is well heeled. Perhaps he was able to take Quigley in tow. Men will sometimes do a lot for money."

"That also is possible," Slade admitted. Dunn chuckled.

"Well, it's your baby for a while," he said.

"Yes," Slade agreed soberly. "It is up to me to try and learn who was responsible for the criminal acts committed, to endeavor to avert more such occurrences and to apprehend those responsible, and to prevent, if possible, any further delays in the construction work."

"Quite an armload," Dunn said dryly. "Well, I have every confidence in your ability to handle the situation and I'm leaving with an easy mind."

"Thanks for your confidence," Slade smiled. "I'll try to prove it not unfounded."

"I'm not worrying," Dunn declared blithely. "Well, I'm

pulling out. Hope to see you in two or three weeks. If you deem it necessary for any reason, telegraph me at the main office in Chicago. I'll send you a wire if anything I figure you should know comes up."

A little later, Slade watched him wave goodbye from the rear platform of the car as the locomotive's stack crackled and the wheels turned over, headed north.

Slade spent the rest of the afternoon looking over the various activities and was satisfied with what he observed. He watched the loaded stone cars pulled out onto the main line above the camp, where they were left with a locomotive attached, ready to roll down near the railhead early the following morning, where the wagons were already assembled.

Quitting time came and the workers straggled in for their evening meal. Slade leaned against a car, smoking a cigarette and pondering conditions. He was debating the notion of putting a night crew to work in the next few days, which would greatly speed up operations. That would require more hands, but he anticipated no difficulty procuring them. A wire to Division headquarters would quickly do the trick.

He felt confident that the M.K. was going to start building south in the very near future, might have already started, for that matter. If so, the race was on. And he felt pretty sure that the railroad building race would tie up with the real chore he had to do, namely the apprehension of law breakers. He was glad to be able to lend a hand to Jaggers Dunn, whom he liked and admired, especially when it dovetailed with his Ranger activities.

As the dusk deepened, he grew restless and decided it wouldn't be a bad idea to take a little ride down the right of way and see how the preparations for continued steel laying were progressing. Sauntering to the upper end of the camp, where the horse shelters were situated, he got the rig on Shadow and mounted, the tall black snorting his approval of a chance to stretch his legs. He was ambling along parallel to the main line when Slade heard, behind him, the hollow, wet boom of a locomotive exhaust.

"What the devil!" he exclaimed to Shadow. "Is that *loco* coot trying to knock off a cylinder head? He hasn't opened the cylinder cocks to blow off the condensed water."

Turning in the saddle, he glanced back as the exhaust boomed again, and again, assuming a crackle as the water in the cylinders evaporated under the beat of the hot steam.

"What in blazes!" he exclaimed again. "I didn't order those stone cars to be moved tonight."

Just the same the stone cars were moving, and picking up speed with every turn of the wheels and loudening crackle of the exhaust. Slade swore in exasperation. Somebody was going to get a piece of his mind, expressed in no uncertain terms.

Forward rushed the big engine and the long line of cars, rocking and swaying. The locomotive flashed past Slade and he swore again, this time in sheer bewilderment.

There was nobody in the engine cab!

SEVEN

HIS MIND WORKING AT LIGHTNING SPEED, Slade's voice rang out, "Trail, Shadow, trail!"

Instantly the big black extended himself, racing along parallel to the moving cars. Slade urged him to greater speed with voice and hand. Unless something was done about it, a ripsnorting wreck was in the making when the locomotive reached the end of the tracks and plunged onto the ground beyond. Cars and stone would be scattered all over the section in a tangled mess it would take many hours to straighten out, and very likely a couple of days to reload the stone and get it moving. Above the thunder of the exhaust and the grinding of the wheels, he heard the voices of the workers raised in startled shouts. He gaged the distance to the railhead; it was frightfully close. But Shadow was overtaking the locomotive, slowly, but surely. Very quickly, however, it would be different as the train picked up more and more speed.

Inch by inch Shadow crept up on the head car, a boxcar loaded with tools and materials. That car, Slade knew, must be reached before making the dreadfully dangerous try at boarding the moving train.

"It's going to be close, Shadow, it's going to be close!" he muttered. "Sift sand, feller!"

Shadow responded gallantly; he was still going a little faster than the flying cars. Slade stood in the stirrups, on tip-toe, gaged the distance to the side of the boxcar with the utmost nicety. Another moment and he leaned far over, reached out and grasped the grab irons near the end of the car.

The jerk when he left the saddle was terrific. One hand was torn loose from its hold. For an instant he dangled by two fingers, with the deadly wheels spinning beneath him. Then he caught a firm hold and swarmed up the grab irons to the roof of the rocking car. Another quick estimate of distance and he leaped across the opening to the tender, slipped, floundered, caught his balance and went sliding down the coal. He shoved his way between the coal gate chains, reached the deck of the cab and was slammed hard against the hot boilerhead. He reached up, grabbed the throttle and jammed it shut. Seizing the airbrake lever, he applied the brakes, slowly and steadily. Too much pressure on the shoes

44

grinding against the wheels might well cause a derailment on the not yet ballasted track. Sliding onto the engineer's seatbox, he stuck his head out the window and gazed ahead. The rails gleamed in the starlight, but frightfully close was the dark void that was the bare ground beyond the steel.

The train was slowing, but not enough. Slade drew a deep breath and took the devilish chance of "wiping the gauge"—applying every ounce of air pressure to the shoes.

The locomotive bucked and leaped. Couplers clanged and jangled. Showers of sparks flew out the length of the train. The bunched cars nudged the engine hard. It skittered forward on locked drivers, its tires grinding shavings from the steel, and stopped with the pilot hanging over the rail ends!

Slade threw the "Johnson Bar," the reverse lever, back on the quadrant and cautiously released the brakes, blew three warning blasts on the whistle and slowly backed the train a score of yards or so from the rail ends. Making sure there was plenty of water in the boiler, he descended from the cab to meet the workers who were streaming toward him, shouting and cheering.

Foremost of all was old Casey. "Be gorry, sir! I thought for a minute you and the whole shootin' match was goners!" he panted. "How in blazes did it happen, I wonder? Air must have leaked from the brake cylinders and when she started rolling down the grade the throttle kicked open. Never saw anything like it before, but I reckon it could happen."

"Possibly," Slade replied, without further comment. "Have the boys set the hand brakes on a couple of cars, and place a watchman over this engine. Anyhow, the cars are right where we want them for the unloading onto the wagons in the morning.

"And now," he added, "I think I'll finish the little ride I'd started to take when I got into the race with the cast iron cayuse."

"You know where you are going to sleep, don't you, sir?" Casey asked. "The caboose on Number Four track. Mr. Dunn had it run down here for the engineer. Sorta rough quarters, but I hope you'll make out."

"I've slept in rougher," Slade assured him as he forked Shadow and turned the big black's head south. The assembled workers watched him ride away into the night.

"I wonder if there's anything he can't do?" observed Casey. "Stopping that runaway train like he did! And the chance he took, grabbing onto that rockin' boxcar from a horse's back!"

"The kind of a boss who'll back you till the last spike is

45

druv if you're right, and if you ain't, he'll set you right and back you anyway," said another voice.

"Yep," nodded Casey. "Except that *he's* tall and good lookin' and Mr. Dunn is short, and ugly as the devil wants him to be, they're alike as two peas. Raunchin' fine men to work for, both of 'em."

Slade rode slowly under the stars. He could always think best on horseback and he felt that he had plenty to think about. He did not in the least agree with Casey's hazarded explanation of the runaway. There was no doubt in his mind but that somebody had released the brakes, jerked open the throttle and slipped from the cab when the engine started to move, to fade away into the darkness.

Which meant that somebody whose chore it was to delay the construction as much as possible had been planted among the scores of workers. Several somebodies, perhaps. Who? Slade hadn't the slightest notion, but he intended to find out.

After a while he turned Shadow's head and rode back to the camp, which was quieting down for the night. A light burned in the caboose that was his sleeping quarters and he found an old Mexican who helped around the kitchen and dining cars awaiting his arrival. A comfortable bunk was made up and, for Jaggers Dunn always went all out, running water was available from an engine tank coupled to the caboose.

Slade greeted the Mexican in Spanish, evidently to the old fellow's delight. He bowed reverently to El Halcón and took his leave after Slade assured him that everything needful was provided.

Slade slept soundly until aroused by the awakening activities of the camp. He had just finished washing and dressing when the old Mexican appeared with a tray on which rested a steaming pot of coffee and a tasty breakfast. With ceremony he spread a snowy cloth on a small table, the room for which one of the caboose bunks had been removed.

"*Gracias,* Felipe, but I'd just as soon eat in one of the cars with the boys and save you this extra work," Slade protested.

"It is the pleasure and the honor to serve El Halcón, the just, the good," the Mexican replied. "Besides, the *Señor* Dunn, for whom I have worked for many years, told me to provide you with the best of care," he added in his precise English.

"Well, guess I can hardly argue with both of you," Slade surrendered, and proceeded to do full justice to the repast.

46

After eating, he saddled up and rode to the railhead, where he found the stone for the bridge piers being loaded into the big, six-horse freighting wagons. They would proceed to Presidio via the Chihuahua Trail, which paralleled the right-of-way. He watched the operation for a while, then summoned Casey.

"I'm riding to Presidio," he told the foreman. "You will be in charge here until I get back, which may not be until tomorrow, according to how I find things going down there. And, Casey, keep your eyes open. Something else like what happened last night may be pulled if an opportunity presents to whoever was responsible for that runaway."

The old foreman stared at him. "You figure somebody deliberately started that engine going?" he asked.

"That's exactly what I mean," Slade replied. "On a par with the fires that have been set and the dynamite explosion which came so near killing a man. I'm speaking plainly to you, for we've got to be on our toes and try to prevent future sabotage of a similar nature."

Old Casey nodded, and his face was grim. "I've had something of the same notion ever since the other night," he said. "I didn't do any talking, for I figured it wasn't my place to bring it up first. But I did sorta take a precaution, as it were."

As he spoke, he swung back his loose overall jacket to show a heavy gun on his hip.

"Took a notion it wouldn't be bad to have old Betsy handy, just in case," he explained.

"A darn good notion," Slade agreed. "And I think," he added, "that I'll have a few more of the boys go armed, just in case, as you say."

"And if I can get a chance at the hellion who's been pulling things, I figure to blow his guts around his backbone," Casey declared. And the way he said it, Slade knew he meant it.

"Hope you get the chance," he replied. "Okay, I'll be seeing you." He spoke to Shadow and headed south.

As he rode, Slade pondered the situation in regards to the railroad construction. A not unfamiliar pattern; he had encountered it before. A campaign of petty harrassment in an endeavor to slow up a rival's progress. Each incident in itself trivial, productive of only minor delay; but cumulative, they could be disastrous.

A method employed by financiers of a certain type whose code of ethics was flexible, to put it mildly. In recent years, Texas had thrown itself furiously into railroad building, and not all of the promoters were all that the heart could wish.

47

To add to the turmoil, more reputable magnates, while reluctant to initiate such practices themselves, felt obliged to fight fire with fire. The result a devil's brew which kept law enforcement officers hopping.

Such, in a modified form, was the situation here as Slade summed it up. Jaggers Dunn would not stoop to such practices; if he couldn't win by fair means, he wouldn't win at all. Such had always been his policy and he refused to deviate from it.

So far the great empire builder had been uniformly successful, a couple of times with Slade's assistance. El Halcón believed that a similar result would be obtained in this ambitious project. But Dunn might have a fight on his hands, especially if the M.K. was back of the delaying tactics. The M.K. was big and packed plenty of influence, and the men who ran it were predatory when it came to business matters. Dunn had tangled with them before, and up to the present had always come out on top, again with Slade's assistance.

Then, too, there were vindictive old Andy Jorg, the wealthy and influential cowman, and the mysterious Gordon Plant, the head of the carting combine that, to all appearances, had largely squeezed out the Mexican drivers who hithertofore had enjoyed something very like a monopoly.

All in all, Walt Slade saw lively times ahead. "Looks like we're always getting mixed up in something to keep us stepping," he said to Shadow. His voice was mournful but there was a gleam in his eye which belied his tonal inflection. And Shadow was not in the least fooled.

"You go looking for it, so stop handing out the sheep dip," his snort seemed to say.

Slade chuckled and did not argue the point.

His thoughts turned momentarily to the incident of the runaway locomotive the night before. It would have been a sweet smashup had he not been able to halt the train before it plunged off the rails. Of paramount importance was the ferreting out of the individual responsible for the attempt. Very likely old Casey would be an invaluable aid where that chore was concerned, knowing the men who worked under him as he did, and by a process of elimination being able to narrow the list of suspects he, Slade, must keep an eye on.

The true desert was petering out, replaced by the semi-arid land north of Presidio. Here there were bristles of growth which Slade, as was habitual with him, studied carefully, taking note of animals going about their various businesses, and the activities of birds, especially the latter, for more than once they had saved him from disaster by indicating that

48

there was something foreign which they feared in the vicinity of their nests or perch branches.

Everything appeared peaceful, however, and he rode on at a steady pace.

Abruptly he turned his gaze to the east. Half a dozen riders were skalleyhooting across the sparsely grown grassland. Their course would cut across the trail a little distance ahead of where he rode. He loosened his Winchester in the saddle boot and watched their approach; this was a wild land where anything could happen, and with things going as they had of late, he knew he must be constantly on the alert. He could see that the horsemen were eyeing him and pointing in his direction.

EIGHT

Suddenly the foremost rider rose in his stirrups, uttered a resounding whoop and waved his hand. A moment later Slade recognized big Hal Murdock, the Barred Diamond range boss. Murdock altered his course a little and shortly drew up alongside Slade.

"Well, this is fine!" he chortled. "Sure glad to see you, feller. These work dodgers with me are—"

He rattled off names. The owners grinned and bobbed as Slade acknowledged the introductions.

"We're heading for town to put in an order for some stuff needed at the spread," Murdock said. "Aim to stay in a while this evening. Hope you'll have time to join us in a snort or two. We usually hang out in that rumhole where I hit your fist such a wallop with my nose, the Churn Head." He bellowed with laughter.

"I expect I'll drop in there later in the evening," Slade replied. "After I see how things are going with the bridge builders. Chances are I'll be in the notion for a mite of relaxation by then. May ride back north afterward—better going at night, a lot cooler. Yes, I'll very likely drop in."

"Fine! fine!" exclaimed Murdock. "We'll be glad to have you with us. We figure to head back to the spread around midnight. As you say, it's better riding over this burned out patch of Hades.

"Me and the Old Man had quite a ruckus over you the other night," he went on gaily. "I told him he was loco as a coot for thinking you were a paid gun-slinger old Jaggers Dunn brought in. Just as I told him he was plumb terrapin-brained for getting his bristles up over the railroad coming through. Told him he couldn't stop it and that it would be to his advantage if it came through. He's stubborn as a blue-nosed mule but he will admit he's wrong when it's proved he is. Just like the row we had when I told him to bring in improved stock and stop relying on longhorns like he was, that folks were demanding better beef than the longhorns can put out. He said longhorns were good enough for his dad and ought to be good enough for him. Took quite a lot of talking to put that one over. I finally got mad and threatened to quit. Then he knuckled under, and now he admits I was right and his better stock is paying off."

Slade chuckled to himself. Yes, Hal Murdock was not afraid

of his boss. In fact, Slade had a feeling that about the only notion Murdock had of fear of any kind was the murky understanding he managed to glean from the dictionary definition of the word. That is, if he ever saw the inside of a dictionary, which was unlikely. And it was hard not to cotton to Hal Murdock despite his quick temper and his liking for a fight. He gay humor was infectious.

"And I didn't feel good about him getting mixed up with Gordon Plant and that loco carting business," Murdock continued, still discussing his boss. "Heard about that too late to do anything about it. I don't like Plant and I don't like the bunch that works for him."

"I see," Slade observed thoughtfully. He did see, quite a few things all of a sudden. Now he understood one of the reasons, perhaps the real reason why Andy Jorg was set against the railroad. It would undoubtedly cut in on the lucrative trade enjoyed by the carting outfit."

"When did he and Plant get together on the carting deal?" he asked casually.

"About a year back," Murdock replied. Slade nodded. That was some months before Jaggers Dunn revealed his plan of the feeder into Mexico via Presidio. Yes, things were beginning to clear up. That was, so far as Andy Jorg's opposition to the railroad was concerned.

"I can usually handle him pretty well, especially if I get Miss Mary on my side of the argument," Murdock said.

"Miss Mary?" Slade repeated.

"That's right. Mary Nellis, his dead cousin's girl. He raised her from a tad, she's twenty-one, now, I believe. She sorta wraps him around her finger. Which I reckon is sorta nacherel; he's a lonely old jigger and Miss Mary is about the only kin he's got. Never got over losin' his wife, years back, and his son who got killed in a stampede. Reckon he'd have been about your age, now, under thirty.

"Understand your railroad has been having some trouble of late," the loquacious range boss continued. "Well, you ain't by yourself in that. Our outfit has been having trouble, too, of late. We've lost quite a few cows, and just the other evening some hellion took a shot at me from the brush."

"Yes?" Slade was suddenly very interested in what Murdock had to say.

"That's right. Funny how things work out, ain't it? I'd just started to make a cigarette. Tobacco pouch slipped out of my fingers and I went way over sideways in the hull to grab it 'fore it hit the ground. And just as I did, a slug squawked through the air right where I'd been a second before. I didn't know what it was all about or where it came from but figured that was no place for me. So I stayed way down like I was and sent my cayuse away from there pronto. A couple more followed the first one, but didn't come so close. I didn't pull up for quite a ways. Over to my left was a long brush covered ridge. Reckon the sidewinder was holed up there."

"And you've no notion who it might have been?"

Murdock shook his head vigorously. "I've had wrings with fellers, but none of 'em ever struck me as the sort who'd try to drygulch a man from the brush. Just didn't seem to make sense, but it happened."

Slade nodded again, very thoughtfully, and turned over in his mind what he had just heard. It was interesting, and ominous. Of course, Murdock could be mistaken in his estimate of some person with whom he had trouble. But for no good reason, Slade experienced a feeling that somehow the attempt on the Barred Diamond range boss' life was tied up with the railroad's difficulties. Just a hunch, but he had learned not to disregard such hunches. Quite often, a careful marshalling of the facts showed that the hunch, so called, was based on a subconscious but accurate evaluation. There was always a reason for any happening although often the reason was obscure, at first. Later he often wondered why in blazes he didn't more quickly see what was plain before his eyes all the time. Could be in this particular instance.

He was racking his brains for a possible explanation when Murdock exclaimed, "Well, there's Presidio right ahead, like an old *hombre* squattin' in the sun. Lucky for folks there they've got all those big cottonwoods growing in every yard. Without 'em they'd be baked. How about something to eat before we get down to business?"

"Not a bad idea," Slade agreed. "My boys will be knocking off for their lunch about now, so I'm in no rush."

First they stabled their horses, then trooped into the Churn Head and found tables. Pickle Simon, stifling a yawn, came over to greet them.

"Just got up," he announced. "Busy night last night. How are you, Mr. Slade? And you, Hal? Been getting into any more trouble?"

"Trouble?" Murdock replied, with an air of injured innocence. "You know I never get into any trouble. You must be thinking of a couple of other fellers, Pickle."

"Guess I must be," Pickled conceded. "Funny how many other fellers there are around," he added sadly. "Makes me want to bust out laughing. I'll send over a snort."

After they finished eating, the cowboys hurried off to attend to their chores. Slade repaired to the site of the bridge approach. He was pleased with the progress made and told Butler so.

"The boys are bending their backs," said the engineer. "I told you that you had 'em."

Slade approached the various groups of workers and complimented them on what they had accomplished in so short a time. Everywhere he was greeted with grins and cordial nods. Finishing his inspection, he walked to the river's edge and for a long time stood studying the stream. After which he returned to Butler.

"As I said before, run your line of crossing at a thirty-degree angle upstream from the Texas shore," he told the engineer. "The line will bisect the center pier, which of course will be set at a right angle to the line. I estimate that four-sevenths of the distance from the Texas pier to the Mexican pier will be the proper seating position for the central pier. That will tend to lessen the impact of the current against the pier, if my placing of the flood channel is accurate, and I think it is. Shortly I'll have more men down here and you can set your cofferdam and pump it out. The center pier must also go down to bedrock and be firmly anchored. I'll be here with you when you start to place the masonry."

Late in the afternoon the wagons laden with the stone for the piers rolled in, having made the trip without mishap.

"Unload in the morning and send them back to the main camp," Slade directed. "We'll keep the stone coming to keep you constantly supplied. I see you have the materials for the cofferdam and the pumps here. We'll finish this chore long before the deadline, if nothing untoward happens."

Slade felt that the last provision must be added, for in the light of recent happenings, most anything could occur and possibly would.

The wagoneers mingled with the bridge men and from the glances cast in his direction, Slade knew that the episode of the runaway train was being relayed to them.

Butler heard it too and came over shaking his head.

"Looks like you saved a lot of trouble," he remarked. "And you figure it was deliberate and not an accident?"

"It was definitely not an accident," Slade replied. "So keep your eyes open for a possible similar incident down here. Right now I can't conceive of anything here that would provide opportunity for sabotage, but when you begin setting your piers it will be different."

53

The engineer's expression became grim, and he swung back his coat.

"Ain't packed a gun for quite a while," he said, "but I am now, and I figure to keep on packing it for so long as this job lasts."

Slade glanced at the heavy Colt which was slung to his left hip, butt to the front.

"Cross-pull man, eh?" he remarked.

"Uh-huh," Butler nodded. "My old dad taught me to handle an iron that way. He did and he was mighty fast and accurate."

"Hard to master, but a fast pull once it is mastered," Slade commented.

"Oh, I don't claim to be a master at it but I can haul her out pretty lively, and I usually hit what I point at," Butler said.

Slade nodded and reserved decision. He knew that, contrary to popular belief, cowhands were as a rule not good shots; mostly noise and smoke. Now and then, however, there was one who was different; Butler might be in that class. He had a notion that Hal Murdock was. The way he streaked his gun out when contemplating using it as a club substantiated his opinion.

"Hello!" Butler suddenly exclaimed. "Look what's coming to town."

Slade had already noted the long line of loaded carts rolling down the Chihuahua Trail from the north.

"One of Gordon Plant's trains," Butler observed. "They'll stop over here until morning, and very likely you can depend on his hellions livening things up tonight; they're a salty bunch."

Slade was of the same opinion, and he resolved to stick close to Hal Murdock and his bunch; he might be able to prevent serious trouble. Murdock had expressed his opinion of Plant and his carters in no uncertain terms, and it wouldn't take much to raise a ruckus between the two factions. And Slade could not see that anything would be gained by such a row. In addition, Murdock's estimate of Gordon Plant might well be erroneous. Murdock, Slade felt, liked or disliked impulsively. And his opinion of the cart owner was probably colored by his resentment of Andy Jorg getting mixed up in what Murdock, with some basis of reason, regarded as a questionable venture. Which it had turned out to be, with the coming of the railroad. Murdock doubtless believed Plant had talked Jorg into it, and Slade shrewdly suspected that Jorg was Plant's financial backer and stood to lose much of his investment.

54

NINE

BEFORE LEAVING TO EAT, Slade contacted the wagon trail foreman.

"Everything going smoothly when you left?" he asked.

"Smooth as silk, so far as I could see," the foreman replied. "Work going ahead okay. Old Casey was scurrying around like a mouse on a hot skillet, keeping an eye on everything. Said to tell you not to bother your head about anything, that everything was plumb under control."

His mind easy on that score, Slade joined Butler and they headed for the Churn Head. Murdock and the Barred Diamond hands were already there, at the bar. They waved to Slade and invited him to have a drink. However, he declined for the moment, preferring to eat first.

"Nothing like laying a good foundation for the likker to squat on," Murdock agreed. "You come along, too, Mr. Butler." He flashed his infectious grin and the engineer, perforce, had to grin back.

"The hellion's a trouble maker if there ever was one, but it's hard to stay on the prod against him," he grumbled to Slade in injured tones.

El Halcón chuckled; he had developed a similar feeling toward the happy-go-lucky range boss the night of their first Ojinaga, across the river."

"That's a notion," agreed Pickle. "I'll think on it."

While they were eating, Butler suddenly uttered an exclamation. "There are some of Plant's carters coming in now," he said in low tones.

Slade nodded, regarding the newcomers without appearing to do so. At once he recognized one as the driver of the rearmost cart of the train he met when riding south to the construction camp, the one who had eyed him closely as the clumsy vehicles rumbled past where he sat his horse.

"Any notion who the big one with the thick shoulders and long arms is?" he asked Butler.

"Uh-huh," replied the engineer. "That's Clate Erwin, Plant's train boss. Mean looking cuss, don't you think?"

"Well, he does look as if he might have a temper," Slade conceded. Then he added with a smile, "But that appears the case with most everybody I've been meeting of late." Butler grinned and did not pursue the subject.

The carters found places at the long bar. Some little dis-

tance, Slade was glad to note, from where the Barred Diamond cowboys were standing. He felt pretty sure, from the
surreptitious glances cast in his direction and a drawing
together of heads, that he was under discussion. Apparently
they remembered him. Quite likely, also, he had been recognized as El Halcón. However, as the carters turned to
their drinks, they appeared to forget all about him.

Butler finished his dinner first and ordered a snort. Slade
compromised on another cup of coffee and a cigarette. For
some moments they smoked and sipped in silence. Slade
meeting.

Although it was only an hour or so after dark, the Churn
Head was already lively, with more and more newcomers
pushing their way through the swinging doors, and the bar-
tenders busy men indeed.

"Pickle's getting rich," chuckled Butler. "But to look at
him you'd think he had just gotten a bankruptcy notice." He
waved to the saloon-keeper who sauntered over to their
table, looking, Slade thought, more like a pensive stork than
usual.

"Business has sure picked up since you railroad fellers
coiled your twine here," he sighed mournfully.

"You haven't seen anything yet," Slade told him. "Just
wait till the main camp moves down here, which will be
soon. Mr. Dunn plans to hold the camp here until the road
is well into Mexico."

"Fine! Fine!" Pickle said gloomily. "I'll be all set for the
boys; aim to make 'em feel at home."

"You may find yourself needing larger quarters," Butler
observed. "Put tables on the sidewalk, like they do in
emptied his cup and was about to suggest that they join the
Barred Diamond hands at the bar when Butler again leaned
forward and spoke in low tones.

"There's Plant himself," he said.

Gordon Plant was tall and slender. But his slenderness,
Slade felt, was the steely slenderness of a rapier blade. He
had dark hair and fine dark eyes, an aquiline nose and a well-
shaped, tight-lipped mouth. His stride was long and lithe as
he moved toward where his carters stood, his bearing assured
to the point of arrogance. An able and adroit man, and a
hard man, if necessary, Slade summed him up.

The cart line owner's garb was out of the ordinary. He
wore a long black coat, a satin vest worked with tiny flowers,
a string tie that was a black line against the snow of his
ruffled shirt front, a broad-brimmed black hat and dove-
colored trousers stuffed into shiny black boots. All in all,

something in the nature of a modified gambler's outfit, as gamblers were generally conceived, although many of them wore rangeland dress or the business suit the cowhands called "store clothes."

Yes, he looked a good deal like a dealer in an establishment of the better class.

That is, so far as dress was concerned. But lacking was the impassive face typical of the dealer. Gordon Plant's countenance was animated. His dark eyes sparkled.

And Walt Slade got the impression that, although he might never have touched a card, Plant *was* a gambler in the true sense of the word. One who would play for high stakes with the odds against him.

His men greeted him with nods and a few muttered words. Clate Erwin handed him a drink, which he accepted with a slight smile and downed at a gulp, placing his empty glass on the bar and gesturing to the bartender to pour a round.

Watching him closely, Slade saw his gaze shift toward where big Hal Murdock loomed above the other cowhands. His thin lips tightened slightly and his eyes narrowed the merest trifle. The next instant, however, he was smiling again and speaking to Erwin in a voice so low that Slade could not catch what was said.

Erwin, who was not good at dissembling his actions, slanted a glance at Slade's table and nodded. El Halcón's eyes grew thoughtful.

Plant downed his second drink, said a few more words to his carters, turned and strolled out, glancing neither right nor left. Slade saw Murdock's brow cloud as he gazed after Plant's retreating form. Then he turned and glowered at the carters. Slade abruptly rose to his feet.

"Let's join the boys over there," he said to Butler. The engineer offered no objection and they crossed to where the Barred Diamond bunch stood eyeing the carters with scant favor.

"Did you see him?" growled Murdock. "That's the smooth-talkin' sidewinder."

"Take it easy," Slade cautioned. "Don't get your bristles up for no good reason."

"Blast it, I can't help it!" replied Murdock. "I just don't like the hellion. Guess it's just the way I'm made. I like folks or I don't like 'em. You handed me one whale of a larrupin', but I liked you even when you walloped me. Plant ain't never done anything to me, personally, but him I *don't* like."

Slade laughed, but inwardly he was serious. He had learned from experience that there are some grownups who, like dogs and children, have their instinctive likes or dislikes. Try to put a finger on the reason and it eludes you like a flea full of hooch. To all appearances there is no reason, but often, he had also learned, the subconscious decision may be more accurate than the logical deduction that dismisses the fact because it has no discernible foundation. Such could be the case with Hal Murdock.

And he did not forget the fleeting change of expression that shadowed Gordon Plant's handsome features when his gaze rested for a moment on Murdock; quite likely the dislike was mutual, and Slade had a feeling, which he slightly embarrasedly admitted to himself, was also based on nothing more than a hunch; that Gordon Plant was not a good person to have for an enemy.

He casually asked a question, "Plant an old-timer hereabouts?"

Murdock shook his head. "Been in the section about a year. Bought a little spread from old Rolf Chambers, who'd let it pretty well run down. It's down to the south of our holding, Small, but good grass and water—close to the river. He brought in his own hands and run in good stock. Made a go of it all right, in a small way. Used to ride up to our casa and visit with the Old Man. That's how Jorg got mixed up with him. Then, less than a year back he started that loco carting business. Have to admit he wasn't doing bad with that, either; but the railroad is liable to put the kiboosh on it. I can't see why he didn't realize that sooner or later a road was going to come through here—been talk about it for a long time."

"Any notion where he came from before he set up in business here?" Slade asked, still casually. Murdock again shook his bristly head.

"Gather from over east," he replied vaguely. "Come to think of it, I don't remember him ever mentioning where he came from. Do recall him talking about the Sabine River country once, like he knew it well, but didn't say he came from there. Also, I remember how the Old Man once said he lived in Chicago for a spell. Educated feller, all right, and as I said before, a smooth talker. Too darn smooth for my money, and I never did like the way he grins. Grin never seems to get up to his eyes. Somehow *they* always remind me of a snake's eyes—never blinks. To the devil with him! Let's have another drink."

Slade accepted the drink and while he sipped it, tried to

58

digest what he had learned, which really wasn't much. Murdock's remarks were undoubtedly colored by his antipathy for Plant, an angle which must be considered.

Plant, it appeared, was fairly well traveled. Slade wondered just what his Chicago connections might have been. Of little significance, no doubt, but the "book" of the Rangers says, "Overlook no detail, however minor, or seemingly irrelevant." He resolved to try and learn more about Gordon Plant's antecedents.

There were too darn many loose threads hanging around, he reflected morosely. Why did the engineer, Potter Quigley, design a bridge that would almost certainly not withstand the ravages of the contrary and unpredictable Rio Grande? And, why did research by Jaggers Dunn fail to show any connection between Quigley and the rival M. & K. Railroad —the answer to another question left hanging in the air. Why did Quigley do it, and who was the instigator? A correct answer to those two questions might put him well on the way to solving the problem which confronted him as a Ranger. Due to his own knowledge and initiative, what might have been disastrous became but a minor nuisance. Which was all right where the railroad was concerned, but did not forward his real reason for being in the section, which was to apprehend certain mysterious law breakers and bring them to justice. Oh well, perhaps things would work out; they always seemed to, albeit frequently attended by difficulty and danger. With a shrug of his broad shoulders he dismissed the matter for the moment and turned his attention to his more immediate surroundings.

The hands had drifted to the dance floor. Murdock was conversing with the bartender. Butler sidled up to Slade.

"I'm beginning to like these jiggers better than I thought I would," he admitted. "Old Andy Jorg may be a heller, but they seem to be all right."

"A nice bunch," Slade agreed. "All Murdock needs is somebody to teach him to *látigo* his temper a bit."

"He got a lesson the other night," Butler chuckled. "Got a notion it sort of sunk in."

"Perhaps," Slade conceded, "and very likely, to use an expression, old Andy may turn out to be not so black as he is painted. Not until you get all the facts at your fingertips can you really form an accurate estimate of a person."

"Guess that's so," admitted Butler. "Let's have another snort."

"And Gordon Plant, he may be okay, too?" he added as an afterthought.

"Possibly." Slade was noncommittal.

59

TEN

As THE EVENING WORE ON, Slade was pleased to note that the cowboys and the railroaders were mingling, chatting together amicably, sharing drinks. Butler noticed it too, and chuckled.

"Feller, you sure got a way with you," he said. "Wouldn't have believed it possible. The last time they were trading punches; tonight they're trading glasses. Do you always affect folks this way?"

"Not always, I fear," Slade was forced to admit, with a smile.

"Then there must be something plumb off-color about somebody," Butler declared with conviction.

Finally Hal Murdock glanced at the clock over the bar. "Guess we'd better call it a night, work to do tomorrow," he announced. "Belly up for one more, boys, then we'll be ambling. You riding with us, Slade?"

"For part of the way," the Ranger replied. "Until you branch off to head for your spread. Then I'll keep on north to the camp. All set? Let's go. Goodnight, John, I'll see you in a day or two."

Slade had also noticed that the carters kept strictly to themselves, ignoring both the railroad workers and the cowhands. He could feel their eyes following him as they pushed through the swinging doors.

The horses were procured and the troop rode north at a fair pace. It was a night of brilliant stars in a cloudless sky, and objects were visible for a long distance. Clumps of brush bristled up from time to time, solider shadows amidst the shadows, silent, motionless, for not a breath of air was stirring. These Slade studied carefully, although there appeared no apparent reason for him to do so. No apparent reason, but nevertheless there was a "reason."

In men who ride much alone with danger as a constant stirrup companion there develops a subtle and unexplainable sixth sense that warns of peril when none, seemingly, exists. In Walt Slade that sense was acute. And ever since leaving Presidio, the silent monitor had been setting up a clamor in his brain. Inaudible, wordless but persistent and very real, it sounded its tocsin of alarm.

Slade had learned not to disregard its warning, so he was very much on the alert as the insistence seemed to grow more strident. And he had not forgotten that just a few evenings before, somebody had taken a shot at Hal Murdock, from ambush. This lonely desert trail provided excellent opportunity for a possible drygulcher or drygulchers.

Six or seven hundred yards ahead appeared a long straggle of thicket paralleling the trail on the west. It was not very broad, but the brush was thick and tall. Seemingly from the thicket, came the persistent yipping of a coyote, which would doubtless keep up all night were the little prairie wolf not disturbed. An owl answered steadily with a melodious whistle.

Suddenly the yipping cut off short. At the same instant the owl's whistle changed to an irritated whine. Gazing ahead, Slade saw something like a popgun ball shoot into the air over the thicket and float away under the stars. For some reason the owl had taken wing, and the coyote had ceased its clamor.

"Hold it!" Slade snapped to Murdock, who rode beside him, and halted Shadow.

"What's the matter?" asked the range boss as the others jostled to a halt behind them.

"I don't know for sure," Slade replied, "but I don't like the look of the belt of chaparral up there ahead."

Instantly Murdock was very much on the alert. "You mean you figure somebody might be holed up there waiting for us?"

"I don't know for sure," Slade repeated, "but it's sort of funny that the coyote should stop barking and the owl take off for someplace else right at the same time. Usually they'll keep on yelling at each other all night. Something scared the coyote, who's evidently holed up in the brush, and something caused the owl to get mad. Did you hear his whistle change to an angry whine? And remember, you told me somebody took a shot at you from the brush the other day. If there does happen to be somebody with a drygulching in mind, we'd be setting quail in this bright starlight, if we keep on riding the trail."

Murdock swore sulphurously. "What the devil we going to do?" he asked.

Slade pondered a moment. "If you don't mind taking a chance, we might be able to bag the hellions, if they are there, and turn them over to the authorities. And, incidentally, perhaps put a stop to the heck raising that's been going on hereabouts of late."

"We'll take a chance, and glad to," Murdock instantly replied. "Won't we, boys?"

61

There was immediate and profane assent.

"You tell us what to do and we'll do it," Murdock said.

"I don't think they would have spotted us down here," Slade said. "We'll cut across the prairie behind those other clumps of brush and come to the thicket from the west. If there is somebody in there, they'll be watching the trail. With good luck we should be on top of them before they know it.

"But," he added impressively, "if it comes to a ruckus, shoot fast and shoot straight. That sort is dangerous as a nest of rattlesnakes."

"We'll shoot," Murdock promised grimly. "I'm itchin' for a chance to line sights with the blankety-blank who took that shot at me from the brush. Maybe he'll be in there," he added hopefully.

"Wouldn't be surprised," Slade said. "Off the trail, and back of the brush over there," he ordered abruptly. "Look," gesturing to the east where the silver edge of the late moon was showing above the horizon. "Should be pretty good shooting light in another half hour or so. We'll hold off until the moon is up a bit. Then the devils should show if they're at the east edge of the brush, where they're apt to be."

Keeping behind as many of the scattered clumps of growth as possible, they rode west for more than half a mile. Now the moon was sliding up the eastern slant of the sky, and objects stood forth in bold relief. Slade called a halt in the shadow of a thicket and they sat their motionless horses for several minutes.

"All right, head east," he said in low tones. They moved on, still taking advantage of every bit of cover. Finally Slade again called a halt, behind a thicket that was a couple of hundred yards from the belt of growth flanking the trail.

"All right, we'll leave the horses here," he whispered. "Will your critters stand?"

"Uh-huh, they're well trained," Murdock breathed back, as he dismounted.

"Here we go," Slade said. "Straight for the brush, and for Pete's sake don't make a noise. If they hear us coming we'll get a reception we won't like."

Crouching low, silently as shadows, they sped across the open space in the white flood of the moonlight.

It was a ticklish business. If the possible drygulchers were keeping a lookout at the west edge of the belt, the first intimation of their presence would be a blaze of gun-fire. Slade breathed deep relief when they reached the shadow of the belt. He motioned a halt and the cowhands stood rigid and silent, hardly daring to draw breath.

Suddenly the silence was broken by a sound, a faint and musical sound that Slade recognized as the jingle of a bit iron as a horse tossed its head.

"They're in there," he whispered to his followers. "We've got only about fifty yards to go. Take it slow and easy and *be quiet!*"

Leading the way, he crept forward, careful to break no twig, to step on no dry and fallen branch, devoutly hoping that his companions, single-filing behind him, would exercise a like care. A few minutes later his keen ears caught a mutter of rough voices; he slowed the pace to a snail crawl.

Step by slow step, the posse wormed through the brush, ears straining, eyes peering to pierce the darkness. As they approached the trail the growth thinned and the ground was splotched by blobs and irregular triangles of moonlight. Another moment and they saw the drygulchers, half a dozen forms outlined in the pale light, facing down the trail, lethally expectant.

A flame of wrath enveloped Slade. The devils meant snake-blooded murder, nothing less. He felt he would be justified in mowing them down where they stood, but the stern code of the Rangers bound him. He must give them a chance to surrender. He motioned his followers to fan out on either side. The move was made in utter silence. Slade drew both guns. His voice rang out, its thunder shattering the silence to shards.

"Elevate! you're covered!"

The forms at the edge of the growth leaped as if touched by hot branding irons. They whirled toward the sound of the command. Slade saw the gleam of a gun barrel and shot with both hands, left and right. And the ball was open!

Back and forth gushed the lances of flame. Yells, curses, cries of pain, the booming of the guns and the neighing of startled horses, filling the night with horrendous sound.

A bullet twitched Slade's sleeve. Another fanned his face with its hot breath. A third jerked at the crown of his hat. He shot again and again through the swirling smoke wreaths, and abruptly realized there was nothing left to shoot at. As he stuffed fresh cartridges into his empty guns, there was a crackling and crashing of the brush, followed by a beat of hoofs on the trail, speeding south. He rushed through the final straggle of the brush and emptied his guns after the fleeing drygulchers. But three riderless horses galloping after the others disturbed his aim and none of the shots took effect. Another instant and the quarry was out of range. Again reloading his guns he hurried back to join his companions.

"Got three of the horned toads!" whooped Hal Murdock, swabbing at a bullet-gashed cheek with a bloody handkerchief. One of the cowboys was cursing violently and cherishing a punctured arm. Otherwise there appeared to be no casualties.

A glance assured Slade that Murdock's injury was not serious. "Hold still," he told the wounded puncher, and deftly cut away his shirt sleeve, exposing a bleeding hole in the fleshy underpart of the upper arm.

"Be back in a minute," he said, and sped to the west edge of the growth, whistling a long, melodious note. As he passed through the final fringe of growth, Shadow came racing across the prairie in answer to his call. He quickly secured a roll of bandage and a pot of antiseptic ointment from his saddle pouch and hurried back to the wounded cowboy. After smearing the wound with the ointment he deftly padded and bandaged it to check the bleeding, which he was glad to note was not profuse. From a handkerchief and the cut-away sleeve he contrived a sling to support the injured member.

"That should hold you till the doctor can look you over," he said. Rolling a cigarette he lit it and handed it to the waddie who gratefully took a deep drag.

"Much obliged," he mumbled. "Feel fine, now."

Murdock protested he didn't need any attention, but Slade insisted on treating the bullet cut in his cheek with salve and a pad. His ministrations finished, he rolled a cigarette for himself.

Meanwhile the bodies of the dead drygulchers had been dragged into a patch of moonlight. There was nothing outstanding about either of them, so far as Slade could see. Two were short but powerfully built, the third long and lanky. Murdock peered close at the rigid faces.

"The two little ones got a sort of familiar look—I'd swear I've seen them somewhere," he said. "That's about all I can say for the hellions. How about you, boys?"

The cowhands shook their heads. Murdock grunted and began turning out the dead men's pockets, revealing various trinkets of no significance and considerable money.

"Share and share alike," he said cheerfully. "Only Slade had oughta get the biggest whack." El Halcón smilingly shook

64

his head. Murdock glanced at him, shrugged resignedly and divided the money into six equal parts.

"What we going to do with the carcasses?" he asked, as he straightened up.

"Leave them where they are and notify the sheriff of the county," Slade decided. "He can ride down from the county seat and look them over."

"And now we're heading for home," said Murdock. "Slade, you gotta ride with us and tell the Old Man just what happened."

"I fear he won't welcome me," Slade demurred.

"Won't he?" growled Murdock. "He'd better," he added ominously. "Let's grab our cayuses and go; I'm hungry."

Slade bit back a grin and offered no further objections. Murdock's temper, he could see, was fast rising to the boiling point. He grumbled and muttered to himself as they rode north for a couple of miles and then turned sharply east into a trail much less traveled than the broad Chihuahua.

"Only about five miles now to the *casa*," Murdock volunteered. "We been on the Barred Diamond range for quite a bit. Runs west to the hills, only this burned out section over here ain't worth a hoot. Jorg's granddad tied onto it for some reason or other."

Soon they were riding across true grassland, and after a bit sighted a big white ranchhouse set in a grove of cottonwoods.

"Jed, you and Cal look after the horses," Murdock directed. "The rest of you come with me. Come along, Slade." He waited until the two hands had been properly introduced to Shadow, then led the way up the wide veranda steps.

"I'm waking the Old Man up," he said, "he's gotta hear about what happened right away." He began hammering the door with a blacksmith's blows, creating a devilish uproar.

A light flashed on inside the building. There was a sound of hurrying steps on stairs. The door opened to reveal old Andy Jorg swathed in a robe. His eyes widened as they rested on Slade's tall form and he glowered.

"What the devil do you mean by bringing *him* here?" he demanded truculently of Murdock.

At which the geyser of big Hal's smouldering temper erupted with scalding steam, a smell of sulphur and language utterly impossible to reproduce upon paper.

"Shut up!" he roared. "If it wasn't for him, I wouldn't be here and neither would the boys. You and your loco row with the railroad is responsible for what happened. Tighten the *látigo* on your jaw and listen to what I have to tell you.

65

For two pesos I'd leave you flat and take all the boys with me."

Old Andy gulped and goggled, and gave back as Murdock strode through the door. Slade bit his lip hard to hide a grin. Murdock flopped into a chair, gestured Slade to another and poured forth his story.

As the tale progressed, Jorg's lined face froze into a mask of horror and when Murdock paused for breath, he held out his hand to Slade.

"Son," he said unsteadily, "it looks like maybe I made a mistake."

"Yes, Cousin Andy, it certainly does," said a feminine voice behind Slade.

ELEVEN

EL HALCÓN GLANCED OVER HIS SHOULDER, then rose to his feet and bowed to the girl who stood back of his chair.

She was a rather small girl—her curly golden head came barely to his shoulder—but the close-fitting flowered robe she wore revealed a figure that left nothing to be desired. She had wide eyes, darkly blue, a sweetly turned red mouth and a creamily tanned complexion with a spot of color in each rounded cheek. Which, added to a pert nose and a flash of white teeth as she smiled at him, Slade thought made a very charming picture. She glanced at Murdock.

"Well, Uncle Hal, aren't you going to introduce me?" she asked pointedly.

"Oh, sure, I forgot," said Murdock, who was visibly cooling. "This big feller is Walt Slade, a right *hombre* if there ever was one. Slade, this is Mary Nellis I was telling you about as we rode to town. All right, Mary, I'm finished with *him*," he added, glowering at Jorg. "You take over and lay him out proper."

"Please!" groaned old Andy. "Don't everybody jump on me at once."

Slade smiled down at him from his great height. "I think you are being unduly censured, Mr. Jorg," he said. "I fear getting nicked by a slug rather ruffled Hal's temper and he feels he has to take it out on somebody."

"Oh, I don't pay that no mind," Murdock said airily. "It'll just make me purtier. I'm going out to the kitchen and rustle some coffee and a bite; we're all starved."

"I'll help," volunteered the girl. She flashed a glance and a smile over her shoulder at Slade.

Old Andy's gaze followed them through the door. "Sit down, son," he said. "I reckon I misjudged you, bad. I'd be lost without Hal, and these other work dodgers have been with me for years. I'm mighty deep in your debt." He turned to the wounded puncher. "How you feeling, Tom?"

"Fine as frog hair," Tom replied, dragging deep on a cigarette. "Arm throbs a mite but nothing to bother about."

"We'll send for a doctor right away," said Jorg. "There's one in Presidio," he told Slade.

"I think you can wait until morning," Slade said. "I looked after the wound; it's not serious. After he's had something to eat, put him to bed and he should be okay."

"Doctor couldn't have done a better chore of looking after it," Tom put in.

"All right," nodded Jorg. "We'll let it go at that. And I reckon I'd better send one of the boys to the county seat to tell the sheriff what happened."

"Just a moment," Slade said. He took a notebook and a pencil from his pocket, wrote a few words, tore out the sheet and handed it to Jorg.

"Have your hand ride to the railroad construction camp—it's only a few miles from here—and they'll send a wire to the sheriff," he directed.

Old Andy took the note, read it and glanced curiously at Slade. "Seems you pack some influence there, son," he remarked.

"I think you can rest assured that the wire will be sent," Slade replied, without further comment.

"Yes, I've a notion I can," Jorg said slowly. "And I've a notion folks are in a habit of doing what you tell them to do."

"Sometimes," Slade smiled, and deftly changed the subject.

Glancing around the big room, he got an impression of comfort that verged on the luxurious. Yes, old Andy Jorg was undoubtedly a man bountifully endowed with this world's goods. There was also a tasteful arrangement and touches for which very likely the credit was due Mary Nellis.

For a while they smoked in silence, until Murdock shouted from the kitchen,

"Come and get it!"

"I'm calling it a night," said old Andy. "Got work to do tomorrow. Mary," he said to the girl, who met them at the door, "put Slade in the room that used to be—Jack's."

In the kitchen, they sat down to steaming coffee and plates heaped with sandwiches and cake, to which all did full justice.

"I'll fetch your pouches, Slade," Murdock offered as they returned to the living room. "And the rest of you hellions hightail it to the bunkhouse and pound your ears. I'll look after Tom."

After Murdock returned with his pouches, Mary Nellis led Slade up the broad stairs to a door which she opened and touched a match to a lamp, revealing a large and neatly furnished room, that boasted two wide windows. Across the hall Slade noted another room, the door open, that was daintily feminine. Mary noted the direction of his glance and smiled.

"Yes, mine," she said. "I hope you'll be comfortable, Mr. Slade."

"I'm sure I will," he assured her.

"Good night," she said softly, and closed the door.

With the closing of the door, Slade abruptly realized how thoroughly tired he was. It had been a long and tempestuous day and the aftermath was setting in. For once he even neglected to clean his guns before retiring. Too weary to even think, he tumbled into the wide bed and was asleep almost before his head touched the pillow.

When Slade awoke, brilliant sunshine was streaming through the window. He glanced at his watch, which he had placed on a convenient table and whistled under his breath. It was nearly noon.

Well, it didn't matter. Things should be going smoothly at the camp, and he had undoubtedly needed a rest. He did not arise immediately, but for several minutes lay reviewing recent happenings. All in all, he was well pleased with the past twenty-four hours. He believed he had accomplished quite a good deal. Looked very much like he had gotten two warring factions together. The Barred Diamond cowboys and the railroad workers had buried the hatchet, and old Andy Jorg had gotten a jolt that, Slade thought, might well cause him to revise certain of his stubborn opinions and adopt a more reasonable attitude toward the railroad.

In addition, and really more important, he had managed to rid the earth of three snake-blooded killers. Yes, more important from a Ranger's viewpoint. And after all he was a Ranger, not a railroad trouble shooter, although it appeared circumstances had forced him into that role. Well, getting the railroad through was also important, meaning as it did prosperity and well being for many people despite old Andy Jorg's view to the contrary.

There was one puzzler, however, that caused him to knit his brows. Who the devil was so anxious to kill Hal Murdock, and why? Of course there was the bare possibility that he and not the range boss had been the drygulchers' prime target, but he did not think so. In the first place it would have indicated a foresight of his anticipated moves that bordered on the uncanny. He had discussed the fact with no one that he intended to ride north in company of the Barred Diamond hands. He could not see how anybody would have had reason to believe he planned to do so. No, they were not after El Halcón, but Hal Murdock. Why? That was the aggravating loose thread which kept hanging around and refusing to weave into the pattern. Could there be some sort of a tie-up with the rivalry between the two

69

railroads, the C. & P. and the M.K. To think that an obscure range boss fitted into such a role appeared utterly absurd. Did Murdock possibly know something that somebody was anxious not to have divulged? That also seemed absurd. But twice, to all appearances, somebody had risked the noosed end of a rope in an endeavor to do away with the Barred Diamond range boss. Back he came to the original questions, who, and why?

Which went to prove that not even El Halcón was omniscient. . . . With a disgusted exclamation, he gave up the problem for the moment and hopped out of bed.

At the moment, old Andy Jorg, holding converse with Hal Murdock by the horse corral, was also a puzzled man.

"I can't figure him," he complained, apropos of Walt Slade. "Anyhow, he's sure out of the ordinary. When Ward handed that note to the telegraph operator up at the construction camp, the feller took one look at it, dropped everything, cut off a message he was tapping out on his jigger and sent that wire to be delivered to the sheriff. Told Ward to stick around, that there ought to be an answer in a hurry. There was; sheriff's on the way here right now. No, I can't figure him."

"Well," Murdock replied dryly, "you sure figured him wrong when you calc'lated he was a hired gun-slinger Jaggers Dunn brought in to do his shooting for him. In my opinion he's old Dunn's right-hand man. Sure looks that way. I talked with some of the railroad workers down at Presidio. They said when Slade showed up there, he changed the whole set-up of that blasted bridge, changed its location and everything. Said Butler, the engineer in charge, did exactly what Slade told him to do without any arg'fyin'. I've a notion that's sort of a habit with folks where he's concerned."

"It was his eyes that got me," Jorg said slowly. "Never saw such eyes—seemed to go right through me." Murdock nodded sober agreement.

"I got something of the same impression when he shook hands with me after standing me on my ear," he said. "Only it seemed to me that they were looking *inside* me, searching out anything I'd rather keep covered up. And, Boss, I was scared. Not of what he might do to me, but of what he might *think* of me. Then all of a sudden he smiled, and I felt good all over. Felt like I'd passed a test."

Old Andy Jorg, a self-taught man and a student of the Scriptures, quoted the words that, written by a moving hand in fiery letters upon his palace wall, so disturbed and frightened a great king: *Mene, Mene, Tekel, Upharsin*—'Weighed! weighed in the balance and found wanting!' I wonder?"

TWELVE

WHEN SLADE DESCENDED to the living room he found Mary Nellis sitting down.

"Cousin Andy wouldn't allow you to be disturbed," she replied to his apology for sleeping so late. "He said you'd had a hard night and needed your rest. You've sure taken the old dear in tow, which isn't easy to do. How did you accomplish it, Mr. Slade?"

"Well," El Halcón smiled, "last night I was the only one who took up for him when you were all giving him whatfor. I expect he appreciated it."

"More than that," she disagreed. "Even Hal Murdock singing your praises like he did would hardly influence him to that extent. But come along, your breakfast is ready for you. I waited to eat with you."

"Which will make my breakfast an event," he declared.

"Oh, there was a selfish motive involved," she confessed. "When Ralpho, our cook, heard you were here, he became quite excited. Seems some of his friends in Presidio were talking about you. I don't know what was said, but it must have been plenty. So I knew Ralpho was going to dish up something extra special for you and determined to share it, even to the detriment of my figure."

"Yes?"

Only a monosyllable, but the way he said it caused her to blush rosily and drop her dark lashes.

When they entered the dining room, the old cook bowed reverently to Slade, who voiced a Spanish greeting at which Ralpho smiled happily, replying in kind.

Mary Nellis noted the bit of byplay and her delicate black brows drew together slightly and her big eyes became thoughtful. However, she did not comment.

They had a very pleasant breakfast together and showed ample appreciation of Ralpho's culinary efforts, which were outstanding. Afterward they sat in the living room together. Slade smoked and Mary Nellis watched him, her blue eyes inscrutable.

"I see you are admiring my piano," she said at length. "It is a beauty, isn't it? Cousin Andy got it last year for my twenty-first birthday."

"Looks like a fine instrument," Slade commented. "Do you play?"

"A little. Would you like me to play for you?"

"I would," he replied.

She crossed to the stool, lithe and graceful. Slade regarded her trim little figure with appreciation. She played very nicely, he thought, and told her so.

"Cousin Andy—he's out somewhere with Hal—told me not to let you leave until he got back," she said, as she turned to face him. "He thinks you ought to be here when the sheriff arrives, which should be some time around evening."

"Yes, I suppose I should be here," Slade agreed. "Nice to have an excuse for staying amid such pleasant surroundings and in such pleasant—company."

"Really, you don't need an excuse," she said softly. "Not so far as—"

"Cousin Andy is concerned?" he interpolated.

The big eyes met his squarely. "No, darn it!" she said. "So far as *I* am concerned. No reason why I shouldn't be honest about it, is there?"

"There certainly is not," he agreed, positively, crossing to the piano stool and gazing down at her. She raised her piquant little face expectantly, and their lips met.

"Now, you've got to stay—after compromising the gal," she giggled.

"Here's to more compromising," he said blithely, and bent over again.

"And now I've got to go visit your rival," he said.

"Who is *she?*" Miss Nellis demanded, a dangerous glint in her big eyes.

"She ain't a she, she's a he," was the ungrammatical and somewhat scrambled response. "My horse."

"Oh, that beauty!" she exclaimed. "Now I know I haven't a chance. I wonder would he let me ride him?"

"He will if I give you permission," Slade replied.

"And will you?"

"Certainly, why not? He's very gentle with those he knows and likes."

"Maybe he won't like me?"

"Generally we have tastes in common," Slade smiled.

"That was nicely said," she decided. "I'll go change."

"Why change?" he protested. "You look all right to me just as you are."

"Ride in this dress! which is short and rather tight and would assuredly climb. Everybody would look."

"I'll promise not to," he replied.'

"Then there's no reason why I shouldn't change," she retorted with a toss of her curly head and scampered up the stairs, leaving him laughing. She had a delicious sense of humor, he thought.

When she came down, very shortly, he nodded his approval of the well-worn Levis, the little scuffed boots and the soft blue shirt, open at the throat.

"Sure makes a difference in overalls, what's inside them," he commented.

"And they don't climb," she countered.

"Hmmm!" he said. "*They* don't need to."

Which made the roses in her cheeks really bloom.

Slade got the rig on Shadow, performed the necessary introductions, cupped his hands around her slender waist and tossed her into the saddle.

"Heavenly days!" she gasped. "I wonder if you have any idea how strong you are. No wonder that poor boxcar you held up with your back didn't have a chance. Oh, I heard about—I've heard lots of things about you from Hal—and I think it was the bravest thing I ever did hear of."

"Hal tends to exaggerate," he replied. "Off you go! Take care of her, Shadow."

He watched her ride out of the yard. Shadow, to whom her slight weight was nothing, appeared glad of a chance to stretch his legs and skalleyhooted across the prairie at racing speed. Slade felt a touch on his arm and turned to face old Andy Jorg, who nodded cordially.

"Son," he said, "you 'pear to have a way with horses, and women. Sorta reminds me of my boy Jack, who's dead. *He* had a one-man horse, too. I'd hoped great things for him, but—he died."

Slade gazed down at the old man who, he thought, was suddenly the picture of loneliness, and his cold eyes were all kindness.

"I think a lot of Mary, but she ain't a son," Jorg continued. "Him passing sorta left my life empty."

"Mr. Jorg," Slade said, his voice deep and musical, "there is no reason for your life to be empty. You are a big man, influential, with the power to do much for others. For people who are trying to get ahead and give something worth while to *their* sons, and who are sometimes in need of a helping hand. It should be a privilege to extend that hand, a blessed privilege to be able to extend it."

Old Andy gazed at him fixedly. It was not hard to see that he felt he was being called to account by this tall young man with the strangely compelling eyes. Life as a survival of the fittest had always been his philosophy, and he had always

74

been able to justify to himself his adherence to that philosophy. But now abruptly he experienced a disquietude that was difficult to tabulate, a vague feeling that this young man had a clearer view of practical morality than himself. Preposterous! He started to frame a tart reply; but the words refused to come as he gazed at the sternly handsome face so far above him.

And gradually in his gaze birthed a certain admiration, the unconscious tribute of the man whose life has been spent in the conquest of material things to the man who has the audacity, insensate though it seems, to fling those to the wind in his search after ideals. And over his lonely soul stole a strange peace such as he had not known since the day his son ceased to walk the world in laughter and lusty life. He sighed deeply, then suddenly he smiled, a very sweet and tender smile, Slade thought.

"Sometimes," he said slowly, "an old man can learn from a young one, if he will just listen, and think. Let's go get some coffee."

THIRTEEN

THEY HAD THE COFFEE ON THE VERANDA, from where they could gaze upon the blue wonder of the eastern mountains, and were still sitting there in an understanding silence when Mary galloped into the ranchhouse yard. Her eyes were sparkling, her cheeks flushed, her golden curls in wild disorder.

"The most wonderful ride I ever had!" she declared as Slade descended the steps to help her from the saddle. "I love this horse!"

"Something we have in common, then," he replied. She glanced at him through her lashes.

"Something?" she repeated and began loosening the cinches.

The sheriff arrived as dusk was falling, accompanied by a deputy and a couple of pack mules. To Andy Jorg's evident surprise, he shook hands warmly with Slade.

"So! El Halcón is at it again, eh?" he said.

"El Halcón?" Jorg said interrogatively.

"Yep," said the sheriff, "the notorious outlaw too smart to get caught."

Old Andy bristed. "What the devil you talking about, Bert?" he demanded. "Outlaw!"

"Uh-huh, that's what a lot of folks say about him," the sheriff replied airily.

"Then a lot of people are blankety-blank fools!" old Andy growled.

"Yes, El Halcón," Mary put in, repeating the words of Ralpho, the cook. "El Halcón! the just, the kindly, the compassionate, the friend of the lowly."

"Yep, that's what the Mexicans say about him," conceded the sheriff. "But of course they could be wrong."

"I figure to add another blasted fool to my list," snorted old Andy. The sheriff shook with laughter.

"Anyhow, I've a notion somebody was mighty glad last night that he was around," he said. "What happened, Walt?"

Slade told him, briefly. Hal Murdock, who had just come in, added details. Sheriff Cartwright nodded thoughtfully.

"Yes, I reckon it was lucky for you and your boys that he was around," he said to Murdock. "Why does anyone want to kill you, Hal?"

"I'll be hanged if I know, but last night was the second

try at cashin' me in," Murdock answered. The sheriff glanced questioningly at Slade, who shook his head.

"Okay," he said, "I'll ride over and pick up the carcasses tomorrow, if the coyotes and the buzzards haven't pizened themselves on 'em."

"There'll be an engine with a stock car and a caboose waiting at the construction camp to run you north to Alpine," Slade offered.

"Much obliged, that will help," the sheriff accepted. You're running things down here for Dunn, eh?"

"After a fashion," Slade conceded. Sheriff Cartwright's lips quirked and there was a twinkle in his deepset eyes. Otherwise he did not comment.

"Time to eat, Ralpho's bellerin'," said old Andy. "Let's go."

Later, when Slade was at the stable for a word with Shadow, Mary and old Andy got the sheriff alone in the living room.

"Bert, just what is he?" the rancher asked.

"You mean Slade?"

"Yes, who else? What the devil is he, anyhow? Dresses like a cowhand and talks like one, sometimes, and rides like one, but I know darn well he ain't."

"Well," the sheriff replied evasively, "among other things, when he happens to be working at it, I figure he's one of the best engineers in Texas."

"He doesn't work at it all the time?" Mary asked. Cartwright shook his head.

"Nope, not all the time. Guess he's got itchy feet and likes to move around and not be tied down to anything. Been friends with old Jaggers Dunn for a long time. If Dunn had his way, Slade would be Superintendent for Maintenance and Construction for the whole C. & P. system."

"I see," the girl said slowly, her eyes thoughtful.

"What about that El Halcón nonsense?" asked Jorg. The sheriff shrugged.

"The Mexicans gave him the name," he explained. "It means, The Hawk; sorta fits him, too. Well, last night was a sample of how he got some folks thinking he's an owlhoot. He has been mixed up in quite a few killings, but everybody he's cashed in had it overdue, no doubt as to that. Don't set too well with some folks, though. They say it ain't right for a person to take the law in his own hands, that he should leave that to the duly elected or appointed peace officers and that Slade must be an outlaw himself or he wouldn't do it. *They* could be wrong."

"You're darn right they could," growled Jorg. "Well, I'd

77

figured to offer him a chore of riding for me, but I reckon I'd just be wastin' my time."

"Yes, I'm afraid you would," Cartwright agreed. "Hard to keep him in one place for any length of time."

"Would be better if he'd settle down and not be maverickin' around and taking the chance of getting into trouble," Jorg said. "I'm going out and tell Ralpho to fix us some coffee."

After he departed, Mary turned to the sheriff. "Uncle Bert," she said, "You didn't tell us everything you know about him, did you?"

"Mary," the sheriff replied, "I've told you all about him I am free to tell. If Slade wants to tell you anything else, I reckon he will. Maybe he will; a woman has ways of getting a man to talk, you know."

For some reason best known to herself, the remark caused the golden-haired girl to blush hotly.

Slade returned before the coffee was ready, to join the conclave.

"I suppose you'll be holding an inquest over those bodies?" he asked Cartwright.

"Oh, I suppose so," the sheriff replied. "No sense in it, but the coroner will figure he oughta do something. You don't need to attend unless you want to. Murdock and a couple of the boys who were with you last night should be plenty."

"They might as well go on to town with you, plenty of room for all of you in the caboose," Slade suggested. "How about it, Mr. Jorg? We'll stable their horses at the camp till they get back. I'll take care of that angle."

"Sounds like a good notion to me," said old Andy. "Will give the hellions a night in town to get into trouble, which they're always hankerin' for."

Outside sounded a thumping of boots on the veranda. Another moment and the whole Barred Diamond outfit, twenty-two in all, filed into the room.

Old Andy regarded them in truculent astonishment. "Well, what the devil is it, a strike?" he demanded. "You're getting paid more than you're worth already."

"Nope," Hal Murdock, who headed the bunch, replied. "But we ain't leaving till Slade hands out some music."

"Music?" spluttered Jorg.

" 'The singingest man in the whole Southwest!' " Sheriff Cartwright quoted with a chuckle.

"Uh-huh, that's what Ralpho says, and he ought to know," said Murdock.

Mary Nellis stared at Slade, ominously. "Just wait till I get you alone!" her look said, louder than words.

From the dining-room doorway, old Ralpho, the cook, spoke, "*El Cápitan* will sing, *si*?"

"Well, looks like I haven't much choice, I can't very well argue with all of you," Slade surrendered. He crossed to the piano, adjusted the stool to his liking and sat down. Booming chords sounded from the fine instrument.

The vibrating strings hushed to a whisper of melody and his great golden baritone-bass pealed forth in a gay old ballad of the range, to which the cowboys beat time and shouted their acclaim, and demands for another and yet another.

Finally, Slade smiled at Ralpho standing in the doorway and concluded with a dreamily sweet and beautiful love song of *Méjico*. There were tears in the old cook's eyes when the music ended on a last exquisite note, and Mary Nellis's dark lashes sparkled in the lamplight.

The cowboys trooped out. Old Andy and the sheriff and the deputy clumped up the stairs to bed. Slade and Mary were left alone in the living room.

"Oh, I forgive you, although I shouldn't," she said.

"Forgive me?"

"Yes, for letting me make a monkey of myself at the piano this afternoon."

"I thought you played very nicely, really," he protested. Mary sniffed.

"Must have been amusing, and doubtless boring to one of your talent," she replied.

"Really, I'll have to admit I hardly heard you play, being absorbed in the beautiful picture you made," he said.

At which she laughed outright. "Now could a woman ever be really angry with you! You utterly disarm her with compliments she doesn't believe but can't help liking."

It was Slade's turn to laugh. "Come over here," he told her.

Mary glanced at the open window, and extinguished the light.

FOURTEEN

THE FOLLOWING MORNING, WHILE SHERIFF CARTWRIGHT was readying his mules, Slade and Mary Nellis stood on the veranda. Her eyes were downcast and she blushed beneath his regard.

"Well?" he said, his eyes laughing. Her color deepened still more, but she smiled.

"Well," she answered, "I'm darn glad I didn't marry Gordon Plant as Cousin Andy wanted me to."

"Gordon Plant?"

"Uh-huh, he asked me to, a couple of times. He's nice looking and has charming manners, but Hal Murdock disliked him from the start, and I put great faith in Hal's judgment, so I said no."

Walt Slade's eyes were very thoughtful. "Does Plant know that, about Murdock, I mean?"

"I think he guessed it," she replied. "Hal isn't very good at hiding his feelings."

And El Halcón suddenly saw the clue he'd been hunting!

"Find the motive and it will lead you to your man," says the "book" of the Rangers. Slade came back to his immediate surroundings with a mental jerk: Mary was speaking.

"You'll be back?"

"Of course, if it's all right with Cousin Andy. How could I stay away?"

"Oh, you will, eventually," she replied. "But don't worry about Cousin Andy. He's just as anxious to have you around as I am. Somehow you have done a great deal for him. I've never known him to be so cheerful and happy. Seems that all of a sudden he's found something really worth living for."

"For which I am heartily glad," Slade said gravely. "He's too fine a man to be eternally dwelling on the past and thereby embittering his life."

Mary sighed and shook her bright head. "I don't understand how you do it—bend people to your will as you do," she said.

"Sometimes others bend mine," he replied, smiling broadly.

"And that," she declared, "has all the earmarks of a left-handed compliment. I didn't!"

"Just complaisant?"

"Well—"

Old Andy coming out the door and the sheriff riding up ended the discussion before it got too intricate in detail.

"All set, Walt?" Cartwright asked. "Let's go!"

"You'll come back, won't you, son?" Andy asked. "Your work ain't so far off and I figure you can spare us a little time now and then."

"I can and I will," Slade promised, as he forked Shadow. "Be seeing you both." He and the sheriff rode off side by side.

"He reminds me of Jack," remarked Jorg. "He has a way of scoldin' you, just like Jack had, that you'd never suspect at the time."

The laughter that is so close to tears welled in the girl's blue eyes.

"Did he scold you, Cousin Andy?" she asked.

"Guess he did," Jorg replied. "And I guess it did me good."

"I'm sure it did," she said.

"Sorta like him, don't you, honey?" he asked. The big eyes met his honestly.

"Yes, I do."

For a while, Slade and the sheriff, lagging behind the cowboys and the mules, rode in silence, which Cartwright finally broke.

"Walt," he asked, "what the devil's going on down here, anyway?"

"Bert," the Ranger replied, "frankly I don't know for certain, although all of a sudden, I'm beginning to get an inkling."

"Figure it's just the usual row between those two blasted railroads?"

"At first I rather thought so, but of late I haven't been sure. I'm less sure now. The M.K. is run by a rather ruthless and high handed bunch, but I don't think they would go in for promiscuous drygulchings, especially of people who are not in any way connected with either road. And that, among other things is what happened. In the acts of sabotage against the C. & P. I can see the M.K. hand, but I can't see any reason for the M.K. bunch taking a shot at Hal Murdock from ambush. Just doesn't make sense. But as I said, I'm getting an inkling of what is back of that. Avarice is a common enough motive for criminal acts. But there are certain very perplexing angles that must be considered. For instance—"

He related, briefly, the defection of Potter Quigley relative to the misplaced bridge and his subsequent disappearance.

"That looked like a delaying tactic on the part of the M.K.," he concluded. "There is no doubt in my mind but that Quigley was suborned, but if so it must have been through an intermediary, for exhaustive search failed to show even the most remote connection between Quigley and the M.K. For a while I thought that perhaps the acts of sabotage were spite work on the part of Andy Jorg, who resented the coming of the railroad, but after I contacted and studied Jorg, I realized that it was really beyond the realm of possibility that he should be mixed up in such skullduggery. He's a stubborn old shorthorn, but one who can be shown the error of his ways. And I can't see him going in for criminal depredations."

"I can't, either, and I've known him a long time," said Cartwright. "But if not Jorg, who?"

"That's a question, one to which I must find the answer," Slade admitted. "I am convinced that the M.K. plans to build south by way of the short-cut through Cienaga Canyon, hoping to beat the C. & P. to Chihuahua City. The things that have been happening to the C. & P. are familiar enough delaying tactics on the part of an unscrupulous bunch. But they must have somebody out here who is thoroughly conversant with local conditions and who realizes that the bridge across the Rio Grande is the key factor so far as the C. & P. is concerned. Once Dunn is into Mexico he should have clear sailing. The governor of the State of Chihuahua thinks well of him and will further his interests so far as he is able; but if the completion of the bridge is delayed, the M.K. will forge ahead. And the bridge is dependent on an uninterrupted flow of materials and supplies. Which makes it imperative that the line from the north be shoved to Presidio in the least possible time."

"And you're here to further that project," observed the sheriff.

"As a side issue," Slade corrected. "I'm here primarily as a Texas Ranger to prevent criminal acts so far as I am able, and to bring justice to those responsible for such acts."

"I've a notion you made a start night before last," Cartwright commented dryly.

"Possibly, although I have no proof to that effect," Slade conceded. "But as I said before, somebody managed to get to Quigley, the bridge engineer, and slide him into the C. & P. setup. Who? So far I haven't been able, so far as I know, to contact anybody who would appear to fill the bill.

"I'll admit," he added, "that I'm getting a bit jumpy over

82

the situation as it stands. As yet, nobody has been killed, although it was pure luck that a man didn't die when that dynamite explosion was set off."

"Most folks don't seem inclined to attribute it to luck," the sheriff observed. "I heard about what you did, of course. I figure that wasn't luck but cold nerve.

"And a strong back," he added with a chuckle. Slade smiled and refrained from comment.

"Yes, fortunately so far nobody has been killed," he repeated. "But such things can't continue indefinitely without a fatality sooner or later. As I said, I can't see the M.K. bunch going in for murder—which is just what it would be— but the dubious characters hired for such chores sometimes get out of hand, as certain big cowmen learned to their cost when they signed on professional gun-slingers to protect and further their interests. Could easily turn out to be the case here. So I'm not only interested in giving Dunn a hand but also in trying to save the lives of Texas citizens." The sheriff nodded sober understanding.

A little later they pulled up on the Chihuahua Trail, where Slade turned Shadow's head.

"I'm riding north," he told Cartwright. "Hal and the boys will guide you to the bodies. Your transportation will be ready when you reach the camp. Be seeing you."

Slade arrived at the camp very shortly, for he rode at a fast pace, and found a laconic message from Jaggers Dunn awaiting him. It read,

M. K. HAS STARTED BUILDING

So the race was on!

A couple of hours later the sheriff and his grisly cavalcade rolled in from the south. His and the deputy's horses, along with the mules and their burdens, were loaded into the stock car, while the men made themselves comfortable in the caboose. Slade wrote a note and gave it to Murdock.

"That will get you passage back here on any material train," he said. "Your horses will be taken care of. Have a good time in town."

"We will," big Hal chuckled. "We're packing along the *dinero* we glommed off those carcasses; pure gravy!"

Slade watched the short train steam north, then hunted up Casey.

"Everything been going along okay," the foreman said.

"And you've been making good progress," Slade complimented him. The old foreman flushed with pleasure.

"Yep, everything plumb quiet and peaceful. Kept my eyes skun for anybody pulling something off-color but haven't spotted a thing. At this rate we'll be booming into Presidio before you know it. Got another wagon train of stone and materials all set to roll south in the morning."

After a thorough inspection of the operation, Slade was well satisfied with what he found; but he experienced an uneasy premonition that things were too darn quiet and peaceful, a condition he feared would not remain indefinitely.

Oh, well, take it as it comes. He repaired to the caboose which was his sleeping quarters to find that the old Mexican assigned by Jaggers Dunn to look after him already had a bountiful meal prepared.

After eating, he went out on another tour of inspection. Slowly but steadily the twin steel ribbons were flowing southward. Already a work train had been pressed into service to carry the men to and from the camp. Carloads of rails, ties, fish plates and spikes rumbled down from the north in a steady stream. The sweating toilers cursed the heat and the dust and made the dirt fly. Slade was passing around the word that they were in a race with the M.K. and the workers reacted enthusiastically.

And gazing eastward over the soaring mountain crests, Slade could in his imagination hear the booming of exhausts, the thudding of mauls, the rhythmic crash of steel on steel and the thunder of dynamite as another army of workers pitted their courage, strength, and skill against the dumb, imponderable forces of nature, and the opposition of their fellow men. The race was on! And very likely, before all was done, the raw stench of spilled blood would mingle with the smell of sweat and smoke, creosote and hot oil.

Empire builders! With ambition taking its deadly toll. As it always had been, was, and always would be. But life lived to the full, quickening the heart beat, sparkling the eye and deepening the breath. Man forever striving, forever seeking to glut his lust for conquest. It couldn't be done, but we did it!

And El Halcón felt that the Master Builder Himself must look with a kindly eye upon this irresistible urge that furthered His inscrutable aims, in the end suborning the evil to the good.

It was with a feeling of deep humility that he turned back his gaze to the humble toilers who had been given under his hand. They were the true "men of destiny," theirs the real triumph, who before all was done might well walk with gods and juggle with the stars.

FIFTEEN

AS EVENING DREW NEAR, Slade inspected the long line of wagons loaded with cut stone and materials, which would roll south at the break of day. Those wagons might well be the deciding factor in the race, for until the railhead reached Presidio they were the only means of transport for the supplies vital to the construction of the bridge.

"Have a guard set over those wagons tonight," he told Casey. "Three or four trustworthy men, armed. We just can't afford to take a chance with them."

"Certain," said the foreman, "I'll see to it right away."

The wagons rolled at dawn, and far behind, a rider on a tall black horse drifted along like a shadow against the gleaming sands. Walt Slade was taking no chances. If he could conceive the importance of the wagon train, somebody else might also.

With his unusually keen eyesight, he felt pretty sure that he would be able to note an attempt against the train before being spotted himself. As the train drew nearer the semi-arid country north of Presidio, where there was cover, he would close the distance.

The sun climbed the long slant of the eastern sky, the heat increased as the sands reflected back the beat of the golden light. Far ahead, the wagon train was a long disjointed worm making painful progress across the shadeless expanse. With Shadow's gait reduced to an amble, the going was far from pleasant.

"Okay, feller," he told the black horse. "Not so good right now, but before long we'll be on better ground. Should make Presidio before noon. So take it easy and save your snorts till they're really needed."

Shadow let one loose as much as to say, "Okay by you, but you don't have to do the packing. *Then* you might feel a mite different about it."

Slade chuckled and rode on, his gaze sweeping the wide reaches of the wasteland. As they drew near the less austere ground he quickened the pace a bit. Everything appeared peaceful. Began to look as if his fears were groundless.

And then, with the first straggle of growth drawing near he saw, far to the east, a series of bouncing dots drifting westward. Instantly he speeded up and very quickly was in the shadow of the bristle of thicket.

Now the dots were taking form, resolving into speeding horsemen who were headed directly toward the wagon train as it rumbled along the Chihuahua Trail. Slade watched their approach, his black brows drawing together. Their progress was purposeful, and he watched as they veered slightly to the south, so as to intercept the moving train.

Of course they could be only a bunch of cowhands heading for town; but Slade doubted it. There was something ominous about their concentration on the wagons. He sent Shadow south at a fast clip, weaving in and out of the clumps of thicket. With their interest intent on the wagons, he did not believe that they would notice him just yet. Another six or seven hundred yards and he would be in a position to dominate the situation if the purpose was a raid on the train.

The seven hundred shrank to five, to four. And abruptly Slade knew his hunch was a straight one. From the ranks of the speeding horsemen, a half dozen in number, came spurts of smoke. Another instant and he heard the crackle of the distant rifles.

A glance toward the train showed him it was already thrown into confusion. He gritted his teeth as a horse of the foremost team went down, blocking the way of its fellows. He saw the drivers leap from their seats to take shelter behind the vehicles, which had plunged to a halt. His voice rang out: "Trail, Shadow, trail!"

The black horse leaped forward. Another moment and he was going like the wind, diagonalling east by south. Slade slid his Winchester from the saddle boot.

"A little more, feller, a little more!" he urged. Shadow responded gallantly, spurning the sands with flying hoofs. Now Slade could see he was perceived by the raiders. Their faces turned in his direction, indistinguishable blurs in the distance. More puffs of smoke. Bullets whined past, some of them too darn close for comfort. But he held his own fire, taking the chance on a lucky hit by one of the slugs. Another hundred yards, another. His voice rang out again, "Steady, Shadow!"

Instantly the big horse leveled off to a smooth running-walk. Slade clamped the butt of the Winchester to his shoulder. His gray eyes, cold as frosted steel, glanced along the sights.

Smoke spurted from the muzzle, the heavy gun bucked. One of the galloping horsemen flung his arms wide and spun from the saddle to lie motionless on the sands. A slug ripped the brim of Slade's hat. Another barely grazed his cheek. The rifle muzzle dropped back into position and again belched smoke and flame. This time one of the riders swayed, slumped forward, gripped the horn and stayed in the hull. Slade lowered the muzzle a fraction more, taking his time, ignoring the bullets that buzzed past like angry hornets. A third time he fired and another saddle was emptied.

That was enough for the raiders. They whirled their horses and went skalleyhooting back across the desert, Slade speeding them on their way with bullets until the magazine was empty. So far as he could see, he didn't score another hit. Which was not surprising. The back of a running horse, even as smoothly gaited a one as Shadow, was not a very good shooting stance. Slade pulled to a halt and watched them fade into the distance, one reeling and lurching in his saddle. The two dead men lay small and lonely on the endless expanse of hot sands.

After reloading his rifle, Slade turned Shadow's head back to the trail and rode on to the huddled wagons. The drivers were coming cautiously from shelter, peering and pointing. Another moment one let out a joyous whoop—

"It's the Old Man!" a resounding cheer went up. Hands waved, hats were thrown in the air. The last few hundred yards he covered were something in the nature of a triumphal march to the accompaniment of cheer after cheer.

"All we need is a brass band and a few flags," he chuckled to Shadow. "The boys are good at making a lot out of a little."

However, the boys evidently didn't feel that way about it and showed that they didn't, without reserve.

"Anybody hurt?" Slade asked, as he pulled up beside the group.

"Nope," replied a voice. "Just that poor critter of a horse drilled through the head. But there would have been if you hadn't showed up when you did. Those devils meant business."

"Perhaps," Slade conceded. "Chances are, though, they'd just have driven off the horses and forced you to unload the wagons and overturn them."

The speaker snorted derisively. Nor did his companions look at all convinced.

"Anyhow," said another, "I was beginning to think darn seriously about the things I've done I shouldn't have and wondering how I was going to explain 'em. I figure they wouldn't have hankered to leave any witnesses."

Slade hardly thought that the raiders would have gone in

for mass slaughter, but admitted that he could be wrong. The way they threw lead at the train showed scant regard for the sanctity of human life. Very likely somebody would have been killed or wounded.

"Get the dead horse out of the harness and line up the team," he directed. "Two or three of you come along with me to look over those bodies."

The dead raiders proved to be ordinary-enough looking individuals, which, Slade knew, meant nothing. He was well aware of the fact that there is no such thing as a criminal physiognomy; some of the deadliest gunmen and worst killers the West ever knew looked anything but the part.

"Recall seeing them before?" he asked. The teamsters shook their heads.

"All cowhand fellers dress alike and look alike," one observed. "Even if we had seen 'em in town, the chances are we wouldn't remember."

The dead men's pockets revealed nothing of significance save a rather large sum of money which Slade tossed over his shoulder onto the sands. He heard chuckles behind him, and when he glanced around, the bills and coin had disappeared.

"What shall we do with the carcasses, pack 'em to town with us?" a driver asked.

Slade considered a moment, then shook his head. "I think it will be best to leave them where they're lying so the sheriff can see just what happened," he decided. "I'll send him a wire as soon as I get back to the camp."

In which El Halcón, who seldom made errors of judgment, missed a bet.

SIXTEEN

THEY RETURNED TO THE TRAIN, which was ready to move, the dead horse having been freed of harness and dragged from the trail. The remaining five could handle the wagon for the comparatively short distance to Presidio.

"All right, let's go," Slade said. The train rumbled on, leaving the scene of death. Slade paced Shadow in the rear, his gaze constantly sweeping the terrain, although he did not really expect any further trouble.

Shortly after noon they rolled into Presidio to be greeted with shouts of welcome. As soon as they had cared for their teams, the drivers mingled with the bridge workers, and the story they had to tell lost nothing in the telling.

"Anybody who goes up against the Old Man is sure due to get a bellyful," was the general expression. "Trouble they look for? He'll hand it to 'em till it runs outa their ears."

After making an inspection, Slade was highly pleased with all he saw. Several big scows had been floated down from El Paso and the cofferdam for the central pier was already rising.

"And we're down to bedrock here on the north bank and all ready to set stone," Butler told him. "Yep, we're going along a-whoopin'."

"Day after tomorrow there will be an addition to your force," Slade said. "They're already on their way. I think we'll start a night shift going. Another week and you'll have railhead here, if nothing happens. Then you should really sift sand. Well, suppose we go get something to eat."

"I sure haven't any objection," Butler agreed. "Let's go."

They repaired to the Churn Head, found a table and gave their order. Pickle Simon ambled over to greet them, looking more dejected than usual.

"How's business?" Slade asked.

"Wonderful!" Pickle mourned. "All your boys 'pear to have taken over my place—I had to hire another bartender. And the Barred Diamond bunch 'pear to have made their home here since you walloped Hal Murdock, and they been bringing hands from other outfits over east.

"Funny thing happened yesterday evening," he added with a sigh. "You know old Andy Jorg has been having a feud with the farmers who settled down to the southeast of his holding. Fenced off waterholes and changed the course of a creek that gave them a good water supply. Creek has its source on his land, from a big spring, and I reckon he was within his rights to do it."

"So long as it was not a navigable stream," Slade conceded.

"Well," continued Pickle, "yesterday evening he came in, and I'm dadgummed if he didn't have five of those farmer fellers with him. They all bellied up to the bar and Andy bought the drinks and they stayed here a couple of hours, having the time of their lives. I gathered from what I heard that Andy had tore down the fences and turned the creek back where it was. I can't understand it. How come he turned a flip-flop like that?"

Slade smiled and shook his head, but it was a very pleased smile. Looked like the seed of doubt he sowed in old Andy's mind was bearing some fruit.

"Yep, I'm sure getting the business," said Pickle. "Your boys say, 'The Old Man goes to the Churn Head, so will we.' " He gave a hollow groan of despair.

"Here comes another bunch of 'em!" he lamented. "I'll hafta go behind the bar and help out."

Slade chuckled. The teamsters were filing through the swinging doors. They lined up at the bar, waved Slade a greeting and hammered for service.

"They'll be having themselves a bust," Slade observed to Butler. "The aftermath of the excitement is setting in and they feel a hankering of diversion. The horses need rest so they won't roll the wagons north until tomorrow morning."

"You riding with them?" Butler asked.

"No," Slade replied. "I'm heading back to the camp as soon as I finish eating. I have more wagons and teams coming down from the north which should be at the camp by the time I arrive there. We've got to keep pouring the stuff to you. Hereafter, however, the wagons, going and coming, will be guarded by half a dozen men on horseback, packing rifles. I'm taking no more chances with this vital link."

Before leaving Presidio, Slade examined the borings taken from the depths of the excavation that would accomodate the pier and found them satisfactory.

"Yes, you're on bedrock and ready for your stone work," he told Butler. "Let your masons take over. Follow the dimensions I gave you and you'll be all right. Ferry your other crews across the river and have them start on the south approach of the pier. I hope we can get that set properly before this contrary river takes a notion to go on a rampage, which it is liable to do at any time. Day after

90

tomorrow, at the latest, the additional force will be here. So take it easy and don't worry. I'll be seeing you."

Having been fed and watered, Shadow was rarin' to go, and Slade rode north at a fast pace. He rode warily, as was his habit, but he did not anticipate trouble. The growth of the arid lands thinned and before him lay the gleaming sands of the true desert. He reached the point where the abortive raid on the wagon train occurred and pulled up, staring.

The dead horse was right where it had been left, but of the two bodies, there was not a trace. He rode closer to make sure his eyes were not deceiving him and that they might have been covered by drifting sand, although not a breath of air was stirring.

No, they were not buried in sand; they just were not there anymore. He rolled a cigarette and considered the surprising development.

"Horse," he said, "I slipped. I should have packed those carcasses to Presidio with me. Evidently somebody was very anxious that they wouldn't be put on exhibition there.

"Yes, I slipped, but just the same I learned something. Not much doubt, now, but there's a local outfit mixed up in these shenanigans. And, horse, I'm getting a notion. What looks to be a *loco* notion at first glance, but not so *loco* after you think on it a bit. One that I should have already considered, seeing as it was under my nose all the time. You concentrate on one thing, bring that to what appears to be a satisfactory conclusion and completely overlook another that dovetails with it. Yes, I'm getting a notion, although what to do about it I haven't the slightest idea, yet. Well, knowing what to look for is something, at least."

He rode on in a more equable frame of mind. His problem was still far from solved, but one aggravating thread was beginning to weave into the pattern.

When Slade reached the camp, he found to his satisfaction that the expected wagons and teams had already arrived and that Casey had started loading them.

"Fine!" he complimented the foreman. "And now I want you to pick out half a dozen men you know to be trustworthy and who can shoot. We'll arm them with the rifles that were sent down from Alpine and they'll ride with the wagons coming and going. I'll tell you what happened today."

The old foreman swore sulphurously when Slade recounted the attempted raid on the wagon train.

"After us hot and heavy, eh?" he growled. "Well, the boys can thank their lucky stars that you decided to ride

91

herd on that train this morning. Otherwise I figure we would have been short a few."

"Not beyond the realm of possibility," Slade conceded. "It appears to be a snake-blooded outfit."

In fact, his conviction that a local outfit was mixed up in the business had caused him to revise, somewhat, his opinion that the raiders would not have gone in for mass slaughter. They might have considered it wise not to leave any witnesses. Such things had happened before in this wild land where about the only law extant was what a man packed on his hip. Yes, as the saying went, Judge Colt holds court on the Rio Grande.

Late that evening a trainload of workers arrived. All good men, Slade believed, crack builders from other lines of the great railroad system, chosen by Jaggers Dunn himself, who knew how to pick 'em. Their camp cars were shunted onto a siding and they took up occupancy with the dispatch of old campaigners.

A certain number Slade detailed to the bridge building operation. The others augmented the force pushing the rail-head south at top speed.

"We're going it," chuckled old Casey, rubbing his horny hands together complacently. "Another week, ten days at the most, and we'll boom into Presidio. Then away to the south we go!"

Slade hoped so, but as several uneventful days of excellent progress followed, he began to grow uneasy. Things were too darn peaceful. The opposition was not giving up so obligingly, of that he was convinced. Something was due to bust loose. He racked his brains in an endeavor to anticipate and forestall it, whatever the devil it might be. He feared something really drastic, which might well prevent the successful consummation of the project.

Because of which, Slade slept little. With plenty of men at his command, he had inaugurated a night shift, which gave him an excuse to be around at all hours. Were an expert at sabotage planted among the workers, and Slade believed there was, he was certainly doing an excellent job of keeping under cover. Old Casey had been unable to point a finger of suspicion at anybody, and Slade himself had had no better luck.

Slade liked to watch the night shift at work. During the best and most fascinating. The glare of headlights, the pound of exhausts and the clanging of brake rigging blended with the thud of spike mauls, the crash and clatter of unloading rails, the flashing arcs of swung hammers in a symphony of light and sound that quickened the pulse and caused one's breath to come faster.

In the smoky glow of the flares and torches, the muscles of the brawny toilers, stripped to the waist, stood out in bold relief, glistening with sweat, streaked with dust; their faces now seen in the gleam, now lost in the shadow. Titans descended to earth to vanguard the star of empire. Their shouts and their laughter sounded wild and free, beating back the stark silence of the desert, flinging their challenge to the wastelands—the roaring battle song of conquest!

Two days before, Slade had moved the camp to railhead, now close to where the semi-arid lands replaced the desert. Not much of a chore when sleeping, dining and cooking quarters were all on wheels. The next and more permanent camp would be at Presidio.

Leaving the scene of hectic activity, he walked back toward the darkened camp cars, making a last round before lying down for a few hours. He passed the long leanto which sheltered the horses, pausing to give Shadow a pat. A little distance to the right was a small squat building constructed of crossties, its heavy door securely padlocked. It was a powder house, where the large quantity of explosives needed for the work was stored. As he drew near he sensed, rather than saw, a flicker of moving shadow amid the shadows. Then there was a tiny flicker of flame, close to the ground, followed by a spurtle of sparks.

Slade bounded forward. The shadowy form straightened, turned. Slade saw the gleam of shifted metal and hurled himself sideways, and down. A gun boomed and the slug fanned his face. Prone on the ground, he drew and shot with both guns.

There was a wailing cry and Slade saw the form of a man plunge forward to lie motionless.

He saw something else! Close, close to the power house was a flower of fire crawling along the ground toward the building.

Slade scrambled to his feet, leaped forward and scooped up the bundle of dynamite with the sputtering fuse attached. He fumbled for his knife, remembered he had loaned it to Casey that afternoon, who hadn't returned it. He started to throw the bundle of death, then didn't. There were half a dozen sticks tied together. The tremendous concussion would assuredly in turn set off the great store of explosives in the powder house. He gripped the fuse as close to the cap as he

93

dared with his teeth and chewed frantically on the tough fibre, the sparks creeping close to his face.

Exultantly he realized that his strong teeth were cutting through the fuse; it was almost severed. Then a rain of sparks seared his mouth. He gasped, endured the agony of the burns and ground his teeth together in one final prodigious effort; the fire was almost lapping the cap.

One more grinding lunge, risking the almost certain explosion should the fuse jerk loose from the sensitive cap. His teeth tore through the last rind of fibre, the rain of sparks winked out and he held the lethal bundle with scarce an inch of still smoking fuse attached. He pinched the end hard, made sure the last spark was extinguished.

SEVENTEEN

SHAKING IN EVERY LIMB, sweat streaming down his face, El Halcón sagged against the wall of the building, breathing in great gasps, hardly conscious of the smart of his burned mouth so great was his relief. Had the bundle of sticks set off the powder house, almost certainly all of the hundred and more men sleeping in the cars would have been killed by the terrific blast.

Lights were flashing up in the cars, heads popping out the windows, volleying questions. The shooting had aroused the whole camp. A moment later old Casey, in overalls and barefooted, came running to Slade, who stood in the gleam of light from the cars.

"What happened?" he bawled. "Did somebody try to gun you?"

Slade extended the bundle of dynamite. "Get the cap loose, carefully, and put this stuff in with the rest of the powder," he said. "Just a minute though—handle that stuff easy—and let's see what I bagged."

Men were running with lanterns. Slade turned the still form over and held a lantern close to the dead face. Old Casey let go a roaring oath.

"That blankety-blank-blank worked in the kitchen!" he bellowed. "Little quiet hellion you hardly ever noticed."

"Just the right sort for the kind of chore handed him," Slade said. "Well, he very nearly made a finish job of it, all right. Would have been curtains for most of us had that store of powder let go."

"And you bit through the fuse!" Casey marveled. "With the fire coming right up to the cap!"

"Well, there wasn't anything else much to do, if I wanted to stay alive," Slade replied.

"Betcha he never even thought of himself!" a voice in the jostling crowd shouted. "Was just thinkin' of saving our worthless hides. All he had to do to save himself was run like the devil beating tanbark. Hurrah for the Old Man!" The resulting cheers very nearly set off the dynamite.

"You all right?" Casey asked anxiously. "You look like something was hurting you. Hellion didn't nick you, did he?"

Slade shook his head.

"The roof of my mouth is a mite scorched," he explained, "but I'll make out."

"Come on to the kitchen," Casey said. "Some wet tea leaves and then some grease will fix it up. I'll take this bundle in where it's light and get the cap loose—no trick, although the sidewinder sure fastened it tight, used wire. A wonder he didn't blow himself up when he was crimping it in place. A pity he didn't, would have saved burying the blankety-blank."

"Just a minute," Slade said. "I want to see what's in his pockets; could be something that would tie him up with somebody."

With a lantern held close, he turned out the fellow's pockets, revealing nothing of significance save considerable money which he handed to Casey with a wink.

He was ready to give over the search as a waste of time when from a shirt pocket he drew a crumpled slip of paper. Smoothing it out he saw a wavering line had been drawn across it with a pencil. At one spot was a circle, at another a small cross.

"Looks sorta like a puzzle of some kind," commented Casey, who was looking over Slade's shoulder.

"More in the nature of a map, I'd say," Slade replied. "What does it mean? I haven't the slightest notion, but I'll keep it and study it a bit, later. Might mean something important, never can tell. Well, I guess that's all."

With a last look at the scrawny body with the wizened face that nevertheless, Slade thought, bespoke better than average intelligence, he followed the foreman to the kitchen car where Casey, who was skilled in such matters, applied soothing medication. The old Mexican who looked after him had coffee ready, of which Slade partook gratefully. The burns, while painful at the moment, were really slight and after Casey's ministrations bothered him but little.

The telegraph office was unlocked and Slade, who could handle the key, sent a message that would be relayed to Sheriff Cartwright. After which, thoroughly worn out by the long day and the excitement, he tumbled into bed and slept soundly for several hours, awakening to a morning of golden sunshine and refreshed feeling. His mouth was a bit sore but healing rapidly. A hearty breakfast and a couple of cigarettes over cups of steaming coffee, and he felt fit for anything.

Drawing the crumpled slip of paper from his pocket he smoothed it out and studied it intently. That it had a significance he felt sure, but what it might be he had not the slightest idea. The line was very precise, definitely shaded at points. It gave the appearance of having been drawn by an engineer or a surveyor, and was indeed in the nature of a linear survey.

Now, in better light he saw that, barely legible, beneath the line were tiny figures, beautifully formed. Also, hardly discernible, an arrow pointing toward the small cross he had noticed the night before.

Yes, the thing meant something, either to convey a message to somebody or to locate some objective. Strange thing for a cook's helper to be packing in his pocket.

Not that the dead dynamiter was really a cook's helper or anything like it. Shrewdly, when he managed to get himself hired, he chose work in the kitchen car, knowing it would give him greater freedom of movement and render him less liable to detection.

In both instances he had been right. After cleaning up the kitchen car, he had time to himself, and who would pay any attention to a swamper in a kitchen car. Watchful old Casey, carefully studying every man working under him, had given the fellow no thought. Well, he had ended up paying the ultimate price for his treachery.

Not without satisfaction, Slace reflected that his own ceaseless patrolling of the camp finally paid off big. At times he had been inclined to think that he was being overly cautuous, was just wasting his time and energy. But the episode of the night before had proven his judgment sound. He still got a cold feeling when he thought of what could have happened had he not been able to prevent it. He pinched out his cigarette and sallied forth into the sunshine for another round of inspection.

Now railhead had reached the beginning of the semi-arid land, and with the desert and its enervating heat left behind, the work progressed even more rapidly.

"Think there might be another one of the hellions tucked away somewhere?" Casey asked.

"Could be, but I doubt it," Slade replied. "And if there is, the chances are his nerves are pretty well shaken by what happened to the other one, and he'd hesitate to try and pull something. Just the same, though, keep a close watch on everything."

"Thought I was doing so, but evidently I wasn't," the foreman growled. "Well, guess most of us has to slip sometime."

"We wouldn't be human if we didn't," Slade comforted him.

"Then I'm sorta doubtful about you being human," Casey chuckled. "You don't ever seem to make one."

"You don't know the half of it," El Halcón said cheerfully. "Seems to me I'm always making them." Casey did not look impressed.

Sheriff Cartwright arrived a little later, via a material train.

"Figured I could pack my souvenir back in a boxcar or something and didn't bring along a horse," he explained.

"About time you were learning to take advantage of modern transportation facilities," Slade told him.

"Just what did happen?" the sheriff asked. "Your wire didn't go into details."

"I'll tell you," broke in Casey, and he launched into a vivid account of the episode of the night before.

"Kept the whole blankety-blank camp from getting blowed to Hades," he finished. "Reckon if he couldn't have done it any other way, he'd have swallowed the blasted dynamite."

"Would have been a neat trick, but I reckon he would have put it over," Cartwright agreed. "Doesn't seem to be anything he can't do."

Slade hurriedly changed the subject. "Going to hold an inquest?" he asked.

"Oh, if you can spare the time, come up to town day after tomorrow or the next day," Cartwright replied. "If you can't, I'll talk the coroner out of it. Plant 'em and forget 'em! Can I get a train out of here this evening?"

"There'll be a string of empties going north in a couple of hours," Slade answered.

"That'll be fine," said the sheriff. "Want to get back to the office, work to do."

With everything going smoothly and his mind at ease, Slade decided the following morning to indulge himself in the luxury of a ride and a mite of diversion. After a few final instructions to Casey, he got the rig on Shadow.

"Chances are I'll take a look at the bridge," he told the foreman in parting. "Should be seeing you tomorrow afternoon."

With which he headed south at a good pace. However, he did not continue to Presidio, but where the trail from the east joined the Chihuahua he turned into it and did not draw rein until he reached the Barred Diamond ranchhouse.

As he rode into the yard and dismounted, Hal Murdock, who was pottering about the blacksmith shop, let out a joyous whoop. It was echoed by a glad cry from the house. He and Mary Nellis both came rushing to greet Slade. Mary got to him first and flung herself into his arms. He reached over her shoulder to shake hands with Murdock, who had become one great grin.

"You old work dodger!" he bawled. "What you been getting into since we saw you last? Come on in, we'll have a snack and coffee and you can tell us about it." He let out a raucous bellow and the wrangler who had cared for Shadow before came to take charge of the big black.

"The Old Man will be plumb tickled to see you," Murdock chortled. "He'll be back before long. He's over to the southeast superintendin' some irrigation ditches he's having dug for his friends, the farmers. Come on in!" Chuckling delightedly, he led the way up the steps, Mary clinging close to Slade.

Finally they all got seated. Old Ralpho, the cook, appeared in the doorway, bowing low.

"The best you can throw together," Murdock told him. "Wait, I got a bottle cached in the office; we'll all have a snort to celebrate. Fetch four glasses, Ralpho."

He dashed into the little room Jorg used for an office and reappeared shaking the bottle, and proceeded to fill the glasses Ralpho brought. He and the cook downed their drinks at a swallow. Slade made his last a little longer. Mary sipped hers.

"Was in town and heard about the run-in you had with those sidewinders who tried to drygulch your wagons," Murdock said. "You did a fine chore on the hellions. Sorry some of them got away. Anything else been pulled?"

Slade hesitated, then told them of the attempt to blow up the powder house, glossing over the part he played in the incident.

Mary's breath caught in her throat. Murdock regarded him suspiciously.

"You ain't telling us the half of it, I'll bet a hatful of *pesos*," he accused. "All right, all right! I'll get the straight of it from your boys when I go to town."

Ralpho called them to coffee and a snack, although "snack" was but mildly descriptive of the offering he set before the distinguished guest.

Before they finished eating, old Andy arrived. Slade was really astonished by the change in him. The hard shell of loneliness and resentment that had encompassed him was gone. In its place, El Halcón sensed, as he shook hands, was a warm glow. His eyes sparkled, his lined face was animated and he appeared imbued with lusty life and well being.

"Been busy as heck," he said. "Those boys down to the

99

southeast needed water badly on their north holdings, and you can't run water up hill. So I've been running ditches from the big creek on my south holding over onto their land. Hired a crew in town who know how to handle such things. Will make one devil of a difference in their crops. They work so darned hard and have so little. Fine people, once you get to really know them."

And Slade, his cold eyes suddenly very kind, could hear the similar remarks of the farmers apropos of Andy Jorg, "A fine man, once you get to know him!" Well, if he had accomplished nothing else, the change wrought in the rancher was ample recompense for all he had undergone.

Also, he believed that his presence in the section had greatly reduced the danger which threatened Hal Murdock. Gordon Plant had undoubtedly recognized Murdock as the chief obstacle to his plan for marrying Mary Nellis, Andy Jorg's only heir, and eventually getting control of the very valuable Barred Diamond ranch and Jorg's other holdings. Now, learning of the change in Jorg and his, Slade's, friendly relations with Mary, the Ranger felt confident that Plant would transfer his attentions to himself; and he was much better equipped to deal with such a character than the impulsive, headstrong range boss who could easily be led into a trap. And it looked like things were beginning to tie up, which was most important from his Ranger viewpoint.

EIGHTEEN

MURDOCK AND JORG AMBLED OUT to attend to some chores. Slade and Mary were left alone in the living room.

"Are you going to stay with us for a while?" she asked.

"I'm afraid I'll have to ride to Presidio a little later," he replied. "I want to look at that middle pier and make sure it is rising properly with no delay. We've been getting a break weatherwise, but there's no telling how long it will last, especially at this time of the year. What happens up around the headwaters of the Rio Grande and those of the Conejos and the Chama, its upper tributaries, is important. The Rio is essentially a storm-water stream subject to great and sudden floods and to extreme fluctuations in its volume. If a bad flood comes down and that pier is not properly anchored and set and above the surface, it could be washed out and we'd have all the work to do over with subsequent serious delay. So I'd better be getting down there for a looksee."

"May I ride with you?"

Slade hesitated. "You'd have to stay overnight in Presidio." he pointed out. "I don't figure to ride back until tomorrow sometime."

Her red lips quivered to a smile, her eyes danced. "Well?"

"Oh, all right," he agreed. "The hotel where I stay isn't bad."

"Wonderful!" she said, the smile broadening.

"But what about Cousin Andy?" He may object to you gallivanting off with me that way."

"According to Cousin Andy and Uncle Hal, everything you do is perfect," she replied.

"And you?"

Mary giggled, blushed, and didn't answer.

"I'll go change," she said and trotted up the stairs, appearing shortly afterward bearing a parcel at which he glanced inquiringly.

"A dress, and some other things," she explained. "You'll be taking me to dinner, won't you? And I'd prefer not to show up in overalls, even though they don't climb."

"So far as I'm concerned, whether they climb or not is now purely academic," he said meaningly.

"Tramp!" she replied, her color rising. "Let's go!"

101

"Try and keep him out of trouble," old Andy begged when the proposed expedition was explained.

"I'll try," Mary promised, "but I've a notion it will be a hard chore."

When they reached the Chihuahua Trail, Slade pulled to a halt.

"If you don't mind, I'd like to ride up to the railhead—just a little over a mile—and see how things are going there," he suggested, and added with a grin, "and to show you off to the boys."

Miss Nellis tossed her golden curls. "Oh, I imagine they've seen a woman before," she replied airily.

"Yes, but seldom such an outstanding example of what a woman really should be," he returned.

"Beautiful!" she laughed. "Keep on and I'll actually believe you."

Her red lips were slightly parted, her eyes bright as they drew near the scene of roaring activity.

"It's fascinating!" she exclaimed. "I could watch it all day. All the glamor and excitement of a big roundup, only more so."

"With locomotives for cutting horses and spike mauls for branding irons," Slade chuckled. He beckoned Casey, who hauled off his cap and came forward, grinning and bobbing, and diffidently shook the welcome hand Mary extended when Slade performed the introductions.

"How's your mouth?" he asked Slade.

"Fine," the Ranger replied.

"Your mouth!" Mary repeated. "What's wrong with it? You didn't mention anything."

"Didn't he tell you about it?" Casey demanded in amazed tones.

"He told me something, very little," she replied. "Suppose you tell me what really happened."

Casey proceeded to do so, vividly, picturesquely, and with fervor. She glared at Slade.

"I think you are the most exasperating person I've ever known!" she scolded. "Keeping all that to yourself!"

"It really wasn't anything to make big medicine about," he protested. Miss Nellis sniffed indignantly.

"He doesn't appreciate himself in the least," she said to Casey.

"Maybe not," the old foreman conceded, "but us fellers sure do."

Slade inspected the operation and was satisfied with all

102

he saw. "I'll see you tomorrow," he told Casey. "Going to town, now, to give the bridge building a onceover."

As they headed south, they heard a voice say, "Well, the Old Man sure knows how to pick 'em!"

"See?" Slade said to his companion.

"Oh, he was just being nice to you," Mary returned. "Made sure he spoke loud enough for you to hear. I don't fool myself."

Slade laughed and they rode on at a fast clip. Soon they were approaching the second scene of activity and bustle.

"Shall I take you to the hotel and get you a room?" he asked.

"If you don't mind putting up with me, I'd like to stay with you and watch the work," she differed.

"Okay, only it'll slow up with you around," he said. "Somebody's liable to fall in the river."

"*Jump* in, more likely," she sniffed.

Slade was pleased with the progress being made. The pier was rising, the cofferdam in place and mud and sand were being hoisted from the watery depths.

Butler came forward to greet them and was introduced. He shook hands with Slade, glanced admiringly at Mary.

"Coming along," he said, gesturing to the coffer. "Almost down to bedrock, I figure. Another couple of days and we should start laying stone."

"You're doing fine," Slade complimented him. "If this weather will just hold on a little longer, we should be all set for anything. Everything been going smoothly?"

"No trouble at all," Butler replied. "Heard you had a mite up at the camp the other night."

"A little, but it didn't amount to anything," Slade replied.

"I suppose you heard the whole story, Mr. Butler?" Mary put in. "If not, I'll repeat it for you."

"Yep, I guess I heard it all," Butler chuckled. "The teamsters brought word down here, and I don't think they missed much. The boys are still talking about it."

"I'm glad to hear that," Mary said energetically. "I believe in credit being given where credit is due."

"Right!" agreed Butler. "Excuse me now, please." He hurried off to attend to his numerous chores.

"The boys on the other side of the river are making the dirt fly, too," Slade observed, pointing across the stream. "They're preparing the south approach to the bridge and getting ready to set the south pier. A fine crew of workers —I never saw better."

Mary gazed at his bronzed face and her eyes were wistful.

103

"Like master, like man," she said softly. "I think you inspire them, just as you inspired Cousin Andy and changed an unhappy man into a happy one."

"I certainly hope you're right," he replied soberly. "And now, if you don't mind, I'd like to ride to about a mile beyond the town. Something up there I want to take a look at."

"Anything you wish, dear," she agreed.

"Anything?"

"Do you need to ask after—well, do you need to ask?"

"No, I guess I don't," he conceded, reaching over and squeezing her hand.

At the apex of the sharp bend above the town, Slade pulled to a halt and sat studying the stream, again noting the high and steep bank, and the water level—now with the river low—above where they sat their horses. Motioning to his companion to follow, he turned Shadow and rode back away from the stream for several hundred yards before again halting.

Turning back to face the river, he sat for some minutes studying the flow of the water and the contours of the bank. And as he did so, his black brows drew together until the concentration furrow was deep between them, a sure sign El Halcón was doing some hard thinking.

Mary watched him in silence, for a while, then, "Is there anything wrong, dear?" she asked.

"Not right now," he answered, "but if the river happens to come down in flood there could be. The bank is high enough to take care of anything but a really bad flood, but if the bank didn't happen to be there, we'd get a lot of water down below that might cause a lot of trouble and serious delay, to say nothing of giving part of the town a good wetting."

"The bank looks strong," she commented.

"Yes, it is, as it now stands," he agreed. "Strong and broad before it slopes down gently to the lower land. Yes, as it now stands."

Abruptly he drew a slip of paper from his pocket, unfolded it and handed it to his companion.

"Mary," he said, "you have good eyes. Study that thing carefully, then study the river and its banks from here to below the town and tell me what you think."

The girl bent over the paper, her delicate, arched brows, so dark in contrast to her sun-golden hair, drawing together slightly. Finally she raised her black-lashed eyes and gazed down the river and back up to where they sat their horses, dropped her glance back to the paper for a moment, then raised her eyes to meet his.

"Why," she said, "this looks like a little map of the river as it flows from here to below the town. Where the cross is marked is right here where we are. Then below is that little bend shaped like a U, with the open end toward us. Then where it runs straight past the town, and then the big bend where the bridge is being built."

"Right," he said. "It *is* a map of this portion of the river, and very accurately drawn. I wanted to know if you would see it as I do."

"And what does it mean?" she asked wonderingly.

"I don't know for sure," he replied, "although I'm getting a notion as to what it *could* mean."

"Where did you get it, dear?" she asked.

He told her. She shuddered and her breath caught sharply. "Drawn by a dead hand?" she murmured. Slade shook his head.

"I don't think so," he replied. "I think somebody else drew it and passed it to him to use as a guide."

"But why?"

"That's a question I very much want the answer to," he replied grimly. "And, honey, please don't mention it to anybody."

"I won't," she promised. "Does it mean more danger for you?"

"I don't see how," he returned cheerfully, for he didn't see any sense in needlessly worrying her. Inwardly, he felt that very likely it did, especially if a certain hellion realized it was in his possession.

"What are you thinking about, dear?" he asked as she gazed pensively around.

"I was thinking," she said, "that it's nice and lonely here and that you haven't kissed me since this morning."

The lack was satisfactorily taken care of. After which they headed for town through the rosy after-glow of the sunset.

"We'll register you for a room and then I'll put up the horses," Slade said.

Mary instantly vetoed the suggestion. "We'll put up the horses together and then register for a room," she said. "As little as I have you, I'm not letting you out of my sight except when absolutely necessary."

"When's that?"

"When you go gallivanting off somewhere to get into trouble. Here's a stable."

The smiling Mexican keeper took charge of Shadow and Mary's bay, after which they repaired to the hotel.

105

The room clerk, elderly, corpulent and jovial, greeted Mary by name, nodded brightly to Slade.

"I'll put you in number seven, Miss Nellis," he said. "Your room, number eleven, is all ready for you, of course, Mr. Slade." He chuckled gaily.

"Seven-eleven, sounds like a dice game, don't it?" he chortled.

"And if you know your dice, you'll remember, seven and eleven are called 'naturals,'" Slade reminded him. "Perfect!"

The clerk bellowed laughter. Mary regarded El Halcón severely.

"Will you shut up!" she said. "You'll shock Mr. Cooley."

"Oh, I've been shocked by experts," Cooley returned blithely. "You'll pack the pouches upstairs, Mr. Slade? Much obliged. Climbing stairs is hard on old bones. Here's the key, Miss Nellis."

"You brought my saddle pouch along, didn't you?" Mary asked as he opened the door to number seven. "Good! As Uncle Hal would say, it's full of woman fixings. I'll meet you in an hour in—yes, the lobby. Now, again, as Uncle Hal would say, you'd better sift sand—for the present."

She smiled at him, a dimple at one corner enhancing the scarlet witchery of her mouth, and closed the door, very slowly.

NINETEEN

SLADE FRESHENED UP A BIT, then descended the stairs and strolled about the streets until the hour passed. The railroaders, their evening meal finished, were drifting in and there were already quite a few cow-ponies tethered at the racks. Looked like it was going to be a big night. He returned to the hotel lobby where he found Mary relaxed in a chair, shapely legs comfortably crossed and wearing a dress he thought very attractive, the color of which went well with her dark blue eyes.

"Well, where shall it be?" he asked. "The hotel dining room is quiet and peaceful—"

"And stuffy," she finished for him.

"Exactly," he admitted. "Then how about the rough and ready Churn Head, which may be anything but quiet and peaceful and certainly not stuffy."

"The Churn Head," she instantly decided. "I've heard about it but Cousin Andy would never take me there; he said it was *too* rough for a lady. I mentioned that the boys took their girls there and that girls worked there, on the dance floor. I prefer not to repeat his reply.

"I've a notion, though," she added thoughtfully, "that now he might feel different about it; his ideas have certainly undergone a drastic change of late."

Slade laughed. "Okay, the Churn Head it is," he said. "Don't blame me if you get scared out of your wits before the night is over."

"I don't scare easily," she retorted. "Besides I'll feel perfectly safe, no matter what happens, when I'm with you."

"Always?"

Once again the blue eyes met his squarely. "Always! Let's go!"

When Slade escorted Mary Nellis into the Churn Head, they created something of a stir. The railroaders waved their hands and called greetings. Cowboys who had heard about Slade and knew Mary, at least by sight, also nodded and smiled. Pickle Simon led the way to a table and even his pessimistic countenance was brightened by a smile when Mary complimented him on the gay and breezy atmosphere of his place.

"Your Cousin Andy comes in quite a bit," he observed.

107

"I sometimes wondered why he never brought you along."

"Oh, Cousin Andy thinks I'm still seven years old and should be kept under wraps," she returned. "Maybe he'll get over it some day. In fact, I rather think he will, and before long."

"Wouldn't be surprised," said Pickle. He took their order himself and hurried to the kitchen.

"I like him," Mary whispered to Slade. "He looks like he was going to cry, but he's got a twinkle in his eye."

"You made him look almost human for a moment," Slade replied. "No wonder, though; you're an inspiration to everyone who sees you."

"Even you?"

"Well, you make me *act* almost human, don't you?"

Mary smiled and did not press him further.

"I like this place, too," she said. "I think I've been missing a lot. Never mind, now, keep your thoughts to yourself. You *could* be right."

Just what she meant by that she didn't explain.

The dinner proved tasty and well prepared, and they lingered over it. Pickle Simon insisted on providing a bottle of wine to top it off.

"If I keep on at this rate, I'll not only be fat and ungainly but cross-stepping, too," Mary giggled. "I think the dance-floor girls are pretty, don't you?"

"Really, I hadn't noticed, how could I?" he protested.

"I suppose it's the wine," Mary sighed. "They say it distorts the vision."

"Your mirror should tell you otherwise," he retorted.

"Nice of you to say it, anyhow," she replied. "I—look, there's Gordon Plant."

Slade had already noted the entrance of the tall, handsome carting owner. Plant glanced around, his gaze centered and he bowed to Mary, who returned the courtesy with a nod. However, Plant did not approach the table, but turned to the bar.

"He *is* nice looking, but I still think Hal Murdock is right," Mary whispered. "I don't like him, either, and, call it a woman's intuition if you will, I can't help but feel he isn't trustworthy.

Slade did not contradict her.

Plant had a couple of drinks and then sauntered out; he did not glance toward the table again. Slade's gaze followed him, the concentration furrow between his brows deepening. Then, with a shrug of his broad shoulders, he dismissed

Gordon Plant for the time being. Turning to Mary, he asked, "How about a dance?"

"I'd love to," she answered. "Nobody will object?"

"Of course not," he replied. "Come along."

Walt Slade liked to dance, and he could dance, and he quickly realized that in the golden-haired girl he had found a partner worthy of his own grace and skill. Without difficulty she followed his most intricate steps. So much so, in fact, that gradually the other couples on the floor edged away to watch their performance.

All the time, however, while not appearing to do so, Slade concentrated his attention on the swinging doors, and on the black square of a window that opened onto a dark alley in back of the saloon.

They were passing the window when suddenly he hurled his partner from him, reeling and staggering, half way across the floor. In the same ripple of movement, he went sideways, hands streaking to his guns.

Through the window gushed a lance of flame. A bullet fanned his face, thudded into the far wall. His own guns let go with staccato thunder, spraying the window square with lead.

A gasping cry echoed the reports, and a thud of running feet. Slade dashed across the room.

"The back door!" he roared to Pickle Simon. "Have you got a back door?"

"This way," yelled Simon, his dejection changing to blazing animation. "This way!" He flung open a door to an inner room, sped across it, Slade at his heels, and jerked open a second door.

Slade dashed through the opening. He heard, fading up the alley, a clatter of fast hoofs. To relieve his feelings he emptied his guns in the direction of the sound, with little hope of scoring a hit. Replacing the spent shells with fresh cartridges, he crept toward the glare of the open window, ready for instant action. In the glow he saw the body of a man sprawled face down on the ground. Casting a searching glance around, listening intently for a moment, he approached the body, knelt beside it and turned it over to reveal a hard-lined face, twisted in the agony of death. From a gaping wound in the throat, blood still trickled. He gazed at the dead face a moment, then straightened up.

Faces were peering cautiously out the back door. Slade raised his voice, "Some of you come and drag this carcass inside where it's light," he called.

109

Men poured out, Pickle Simon first of all, a cocked, sawed-off in his hand.

"Just a minute," Slade told him and hurried inside to look for Mary Nellis. She ran to him with a glad cry.

"You all right, darling?" she sobbed.

"I'm okay," Slade replied. "Hope I didn't stand you on your head when I threw you away from me—had to get you out of line."

"Not quite," she said, adding with a wan smile, "I sure did some cross-stepping, though."

"I'm glad you didn't faint, and fall," he said.

"Faint!" with as near a snort as a musical feminine voice could achieve, "women brought up on the Big Bend rangeland don't faint easily. As soon as I saw you were all right I wasn't worried anymore. Did you get the—the—I won't say it, but I'll think it?"

"One of them, there were two," he replied. "They're bringing him inside now, what's left of him."

The blue eyes blazed. "I hope there isn't much," she said. "And the other one got away?"

"I'm afraid so," he admitted. "We'll search the alley later, but I'm pretty sure he got in the clear—he had a horse up the alley. Come back to the table, now, and wait for me. You're a girl to ride the river with!"

She flushed with pleasure at the highest compliment the rangeland can pay.

The body had been dragged into the back room, where men were grouped about it, exclaiming, gesturing.

"The hellion's been here before," Pickle Simon declared. "I can't remember who with, but he's been here. I'll swear to it, Mr. Slade."

The Ranger nodded. His face was set in granite lines, his eyes were terrible. The callous devils had risked killing the girl to chance a shot at him. Looked like he was up against as snake-blooded a bunch as had been the late Veck Sosna, killed by Slade in an Amarillo gunfight, and his ruthless Comancheros.

And there was no doubt in Slade's mind as to whom the dead killer had been with in the Churn Head.

For in the blaze of the gun outside the window he had glimpsed a face, the face of Clate Erwin, Gordon Plant's *carting boss!*

110

TWENTY

"WHAT SHALL WE DO WITH THE CARCASS?" Pickle asked.

"Lay it over to one side and cover it with a blanket," Slade directed. "In the morning I'll wire the sheriff and he can come down and take care of it."

"He's a busy man nowadays," Pickle observed cheerfully. "Well, the more of this kind for him to take care of, the better off we'll all be. You did a fine chore, Mr. Slade, a mighty fine chore."

There was a general and hearty assent.

Satisfied that everything was under control, Slade went back to Mary, to find her completely recovered from the harrowing experince. Her lips were red, her eyes wide and sparkling.

"Do you think I'm terrible?" she asked. "But really, I like this place better than ever."

"I think you're wonderful," he said, and meant it. She laughed gaily.

"Here comes Mr. Simon with another bottle of wine," she said. "I'm glad, even if I am terrible, I feel another drink will go fine right now, don't you?"

"I certainly do," he agreed heartily.

Pickle filled the glasses with a flourish, including one for himself, which he raised in salute.

"Here's to good hunting, Mr. Slade," he said and swallowed the drink with mighty gusto and relish.

"All of a sudden he looks really happy," Mary whispered to Slade as the saloon-keeper ambled off. "I think he likes excitement, too."

Abruptly her big eyes were serious, and a moment later she gave El Halcón something of a start.

"Walt," she asked, "do you know who tried to have you killed tonight?"

Slade knew, but he countered with a question of his own, "Who?"

Mary regarded him a moment, then lowering her voice, said very slowly, "Gordon Plant."

Slade dissembled his surprise. "Do you really think so?" he asked.

"I don't think, I know," she replied. "When he looked at you when he came in a little while ago, there was death in

111

his face. I didn't mention it to you at the time, fearing that you would think me absurd.

"And," she added with a burst of inspiration, "I'll wager it was he who tried to kill Hal Murdock."

Walt Slade decided it was no time for subterfuge. "Right on both counts," he agreed. "But, Mary, please don't speak of it to anybody."

"I won't, if you ask me not to, and I guess you already have," she promised. She shuddered. "But you'll be in constant danger so long as he's alive."

"Not nearly so much, now that I know whom to keep an eye on," he comforted her. "So don't worry your pretty head about it."

"I pray God there won't, but if anything does happen to you, Gordon Plant won't live long, that I promise you," she said.

Looking at her, Slade had no doubt but that she meant just what she said, and that it was doubly important for *him* to try and stay alive.

As he sipped his wine, Slade wondered if Clate Erwin knew that he, Slade, had seen his face outside the window. If so, the carting boss would very likely make himself scarce for a while. A search of the alley had revealed nothing other than evidence that horses had been tethered there for some time. Evidently the one the dead gun-slinger rode had followed the other when Erwin hightailed. Well, it didn't matter much, one way or the other. Erwin was just a hired hand obeying orders; Plant was the man to watch.

The exhiliration induced by the stirring happenings, added to the red-eye consumed, was getting results. Everybody seemed talking at once, and not sotto voice. The resulting din was deafening.

"Wheew!" Mary exclaimed. "One can't hear oneself think."

"How about hitting the outside for a while?" Slade suggested. "I think maybe you might like to take a look at the work on the bridge—we have a night shift going now."

"That would be wonderful," she replied. "Let's go."

They said goodnight to Pickle and strolled out, admiring glances following them. Under the silver glow of the stars they walked slowly to where the bridge builders filled the night with the music of steel on steel. Mary's eyes were wide and bright as she surveyed the orderly confusion in the light of the torches and the flares.

"Men have all the best of it!" she lamented. "This is what
112

I call really living. Watching them and what they are accomplishing makes me feel utterly futile."

"There is usually a woman behind the man to inspire him to accomplishment," Slade reminded gently. "Don't forget that."

"You always seem to have the right answer," she said, her smile a little tremulous. A moment later she asked, "Is there something wrong, dear? You look serious."

"I was listening to the sound the river is making," he answered. "Can you hear it—a low moaning sound?"

"Why yes, now that you mention it, I do," she replied. "What does it mean?"

"It means," he explained, "that the river is rising, very slowly, so far, but rising nethertheless."

"And that means trouble for you?"

"It could," he acknowledged. "That is, if it rises too much. I'll get in touch with El Paso, by wire, in the morning and try and learn of weather conditions up around the headwaters of the Rio Grande and its tributaries. This has been a very hot spring and the Rio gets much of its water from the Colorado mountains, from the melting snow. Add a few heavy rains to that and she's liable to go on a rampage, and a real flood condition on the Rio is something to reckon with. It would slow up the work here, badly."

"I see," she said thoughtfully. "Let's hope it won't be too bad."

"We'll take precautions against any eventuality and make out okay," he assured her.

They walked around a while longer watching the work. Slade glanced down at his companion.

"Getting tired?" he asked.

"A little," she admitted. "It's been a busy day."

"Then suppose we call it a night," he suggested, turning their steps toward the hotel.

Mary smiled and slanted him a glance through her lashes, but did not otherwise comment.

The following morning, fairly early, Slade and the girl rode north. "I'd like to visit the camp first and see how things there are coming along," he said.

"The longest way is the best way," she replied blithely. "Then I suppose you'll ride back to Presidio."

"Yes," he agreed. "I want to keep an eye on that river, but I'll be closer to the ranchhouse from now on; you'll be seeing me."

"I'd better, or I'll come looking for you," she threatened.

"Expect I wouldn't be hard to find, especially as I'd be looking for you," he said.

They found everything going smoothly at the railhead. He sent a wire to Sheriff Cartwright, another to El Paso asking about weather conditions to the north, and after he had looked things over, they headed for the Barred Diamond *casa*, which they reached without incident.

"Well, have a nice time, honey?" old Andy asked Mary while Slade was securing Shadow a helping of oats before the trip back to the bridge.

"Cousin Andy," she replied, "I feel just like a contented tabby cat."

"Hmmm! Cats have claws," Jorg observed. "I hope you didn't use 'em on him too much."

Mary blushed and did not answer.

The sheriff arrived before dark and he and Slade went into conference.

"Okay," Cartwright said in conclusion, "I'll be ready whenever you want me. Good hunting!"

Three days later the railhead boomed into Presidio and the high iron was joined with the tracks already laid on the bridge approach. Close behind was a trainload of steel for the bridge spans. The north pier stood solid and secure and the steel workers at once got busy with the first span. Timber supports were reared and the finger of steel crept slowly toward the firmly anchored and almost completed middle pier.

But now the Rio Grande was beginning to sit up and take notice, and Slade had an uneasy feeling that Ol' Debbil River didn't approve of such goings on. The answers to his wires inquiring about weather conditions to the north were disquieting. There were heavy rains around the headwaters of the main stream and its tributaries, and the snow on the mountains was melting at an unusually fast rate. The river was rising, still slowly, but steadily.

"Once we get the girders onto the center pier it will hold no matter how much water comes down," Slade told Butler. "But any delay right now could cause us plenty of trouble."

He turned and gazed to the northwest as he spoke, where at the sharp bend above the town, the flood water was chafing against the high bank.

"We'll do it," Butler declared confidently. "I never saw men work like ours are. It isn't just the bonus money you

114

promised them. They say to hell with that, the Old Man wants this bridge up in a hurry, and that's just the way he's going to get it—in a hurry, if we have to bust our cinches to do it. Nobody's going to let *him* down!"

"Yes, they're a fine bunch," Slade agreed. "And I'm certainly not going to let *them* down," he added grimly, his gaze still fixed on the distant bend.

Butler glanced at him inquiringly, but Slade did not elaborate his remark.

The river continued to rise. Now its moan was approaching the snarl of a predatory animal stalking a helpless victim. The bridge workers redoubled their efforts and the steel fingers clawed toward the massive middle pier. The south approach was ready, the south pier stood waiting.

"Four more days and we'll do it," said Butler. "And not a minute too soon."

Slade nodded grim assent, and gazed toward the bend above the town. And over the wires clicked an ominous message,

CLOUDBURST TO THE NORTH.
CONEJOS AND CHAMA OVERFLOWING
BANKS.

"And that," Slade told the engineer, "could mean trouble. Anything interrupting the progress of the work right now might well be disastrous. That center pier is due to receive a vicious battering when the full force of the flood reaches here. With the girders anchoring it firmly, there'll be nothing to worry about, otherwise I'm not too sure. You can never be certain as to just what will happen with water hammering the masonry above the point of moment, and such a flood as will very likely strike here will probably flow water over the top of the stone. Well, we'll see."

Hard on the heels of the first message came a second, very laconic, from Jaggers Dunn,

AM ON MY WAY.

"He always likes to be in on the finish," Slade chuckled as he passed the wire to Butler. "Well, this time he's liable to see fireworks."

As the afternoon waned and the shadows grew long, Slade remarked to the engineer, "Everything appears to be under control and I don't anticipate any trouble in the next forty-eight hours at the earliest, so I think I'll ride over to the Barred Diamond *casa*."

"Go to it," said Butler. "You've sure earned a bit of rest. Don't worry, I'll look after everything and send you word if I think you're really needed here."

"Okay, then, and thanks," Slade replied. "I'll be seeing you tomorrow."

That night, as they sat together in the ranchhouse living room after old Andy had ambled off to bed, Mary Nellis was silent and distraught, her blue eyes regarding Slade wistfully. He knew that she had something on her mind and waited for it to be divulged.

"Walt," she said suddenly, "just what are you and why are you here?"

"Well, I'm trying to build a railroad, am I not?" he countered.

"Yes," she conceded. "Again you can call it a woman's intuition, but I have a strong feeling that you are here for something else, for something perhaps more important even than building a railroad. Why did Gordon Plant try to kill you? Because of me? No. Hal Murdock, yes, because he figured Hal was doing his best to keep us apart, but not you. I give him credit for being smart enough to realize that I would never marry him under any circumstances. So that was not his motive. Why does he figure you are in his way?"

Slade regarded her in silence for a moment. Then he slipped something from a cunningly concealed secret pocket in his broad leather belt and handed it to her—a gleaming silver star set on a silver circle, the feared and honored badge of the Texas Rangers. She gazed at it a moment, then handed it back to him.

"So that's it," she said. "I can't say I'm overly surprised. For some time I believed you to be something like that, and you are everything a Texas Ranger is supposed to be and usually is, according to all I've heard of them. And you are here because of the trouble the railroad has been having, and you believe Gordon Plant is responsible for the trouble?"

"Yes to both questions," he replied. "I was sent here to investigate criminal acts committed against the railroad. And I am convinced that Gordon Plant is primarily responsible for those acts. He is an agent, I am sure, of the M.K. Railroad, the C. & P.'s great business rival, sent here to delay the C. & P. building program in the interest of the other road. And I am just as sure that he has gone a great deal farther than his employers ever intended him to, that he has gotten completely out of hand and is prepared to go to

116

any lengths to advance his own personal interests. Something similar to what happened to certain reputable cattlemen who put questionable characters on their payrolls. Misplacing that bridge where it would almost certainly be washed out by flood water, while decidedly unethical, to put it mildly, would be considered by unscrupulous financiers a permissible and effective delaying tactic. But not such an eruption of violence as Plant has instigated. Only sheer luck had prevented those acts from resulting in murder."

"I think the railroad workers would be inclined to credit it to something other than luck," Mary interrupted dryly. Slade smiled, and let that pass.

"Plant knows that the M.K. people can't come out and repudiate him without tipping their own hand," he continued. "In fact, the M.K. is in the position of the gentleman who got the bear by the tail; they'd doubtless like to let go, but can't. But if Plant isn't stopped soon, very probably some innocent person or persons will die."

"Can't you arrest him, or have Sheriff Cartwright arrest him?" she asked. Slade smiled ruefully and shook his head.

"Unfortunately I have not one iota of proof that Plant is responsible," he replied. "I recognized his carting boss, Clate Erwin, as one of the men who tried to shoot me through the Churn Head window the other night, but that would be just my word against Erwin's. And to try to get a jury to believe you recognized a man by the flash of a gun outside a dark window, with a good defense lawyer tearing your story to pieces, would be a dubious chore to say the least. And even if it were put over, there would still be nothing against Plant. He could repudiate Erwin if Erwin said he was told by Plant to shoot me, and make it stick.

"Plant is the most difficult type for a law enforcement officer to apprehend. He is a shadow, with the rare gift of always being unobtrusive. The other night was the first time he ever definitely entered the picture, and that largely by chance. Heretofore he has always managed to keep in the background, scheming, directing, but never tipping his hand."

Mary shuddered. "And in the meanwhile you are in constant danger."

"As I told you before, not so much now that I know whom to keep an eye on," he replied. "And I think *Señor* Plant's career of whimsy is drawing to a close," he added grimly.

"I hope so," she sighed. "And then—I suppose you'll be leaving."

"Yes, I'll have to make a run back to the Post to see what Captain Jim has lined up for me," he admitted. "Doesn't mean I have to stay there, especially with attractions—elsewhere."

"If the attraction is strong enough," she smiled. "Well, I'll do my best." She glanced at the stairs.

TWENTY-ONE

THE NEXT DAY SLADE WIRED A cryptic message to Sheriff Cartwright. As a result, in the dead of night the sheriff and half a dozen deputies and their horses arrived via a material train, and went into seclusion with Casey and the old Mexican who looked after Slade, to take care of their wants. Nobody else knew they were at the camp.

"I'm sure tomorrow night will be it, in the nature of a last resort," Slade told Cartwright. "By then the river will be at crest and a real breakthrough could cause tremendous damage here, perhaps delay the work indefinitely. At any rate long enough for the M.K. to get a real head start and win the race to Chihuahua City. Yes, I'm confident they'll try it at the upper bend. They must have had it planned for quite a while. That little snake who tried to blow up the powder house wasn't packing that plat of the river for nothing."

"You don't think they may suspect you have figured out what they plan to do?" asked the sheriff. Slade shook his head.

"I really don't think so," he replied. "If they have figured it, they will have taken precautions and the hunter may turn out to be the hunted."

"A nice prospect," grunted Cartwright. "Well, guess we'll have to risk it; that's always the way in this sort of game."

"And we'll work on the premise that they may have possibly caught on and try to guard against such an eventuality," Slade replied. "Is everything understood now?"

"Yep," answered the sheriff. "All set to go."

"Okay, I'll see you tomorrow night—tonight, rather, it's past midnight. Now I'm going to try and get a little sleep, and you'd better, too. *Beunas noches!*"

All the following day the river rose steadily, growling and grumbling, chaffing its banks, thundering against the massive center pier, while the bridge builders worked with frantic speed to anchor the pier with the forward reaching span. The thud of hammers, the chatter of riveters, the creaking of the cranes and the rhythmic clang of steel on steel rose above the loudening complaint of the swollen stream.

"We're doing it," enthused Butler. "Before tomorrow morning the span will be in place and nothing more to worry about."

"I hope so," Slade replied. "Yes, I think we will, if nothing goes wrong."

He turned and gazed upstream as he spoke, where shone the gleam of the rushing water charging around the bend, almost cresting the high bank. Butler gazed also, apprehensively. For Slade had taken the engineer into his confidence.

"We'll stop the hellions, if they do try something," he growled. "When do you figure to leave the camp?"

"Be ready to move a couple of hours after dark," Slade replied. "I figure they'll hardly try anything before ten o'clock. Most likely if they do at all it will be after midnight; but we can't afford to take chances."

"I'll be ready," Butler promised. "I'm itching for a crack at those devils."

The afternoon wore on, with the river rising and the work progressing at a steady pace. Slade began to feel optimistic as to the outcome. Unless something totally unexpected happened the real consummation of the project was at hand. And it was up to him to prevent that "unexpected something" from happening.

Slade was everywhere, directing, encouraging, solving problems that rose with smooth efficiency. The men greeted him with cheers and waving hands and bent their brawny backs. Darkness fell and the flares and torches glared back at the stars blossoming in the sky, with only a thin wisping of cloud to dim their brightness. There would be no moon until very late.

Which fitted well with El Halcón's purpose. The prairie would be shadowy with little chance that moving objects would be spotted from any distance.

Slade made a final tour of inspection and decided that there was nothing that Casey could not handle by himself. He located Butler and together they repaired to the camp car where the sheriff and his posse were holed up. Otherwise the camp was deserted, save for the old Mexican who bade them *"Vaya usted con Dios"*—Go you with God.

Getting the rigs on their horses they rode north on the Chihuahua Trail, and as they rode Slade outlined his plan.

"We'll ride north for a couple of miles, then turn west and make a wide circle back to the river," he told them. "Not far back from the apex of the bend is a straggle of chaparral. There we'll hole up and wait. If they show, we should be able to get the drop on them. But remember, I'm not at all sure that they will give up without a fight. Plant is a desperate man and those he will have with him are of the same ilk. I figure only his trusted, close-knit bunch will accompany him on this chore, and they're plenty salty. But those are the ones we want. I doubt if many of his carters are in his operation against the railroad. Perhaps not all, if any, of his cowhands. What we'll be up against is the cream of the crop, so if it comes to a corpse-and-cartridge session, shoot fast and shoot straight."

"What if the hellions have caught on and are in that brush waiting for us?" one of the deputies asked nervously.

"Then you'll know they're there when you see the flash of their guns," Slade replied dryly. "Chances are you won't hear the reports, lead traveling a mite faster than sound."

"Gosh!" muttered the deputy. Hardbitten old Sheriff Cartwright chuckled.

Just the same it was nerve racking work, riding slowly toward the dark and silent loom of the thicket, not knowing that at any moment they would be met by a blaze of gunfire. It was with a general sigh of relief that they reached the edge of the chaparral with nothing happening. The posse dismounted, the horses were tethered and the tedious wait began.

"Have that bundle of oil-soaked cotton waste to the front," Slade directed. "Touch the match to it when I give the word. It'll flare up instantly and should help throw them off balance besides giving us good shooting light. All right, everybody, quiet from now on and keep your ears and eyes open."

Slowly the hours passed. The great clock in the sky wheeled westward. Midnight came and went and Slade began to wonder if he had guessed wrong. Was starting to look that way.

Then suddenly his keen ears caught a sound, a muffled, persistent sound that steadily loudened—the beat of horses' hoofs on the soft ground near the river.

"Get set!" he whispered to his companions. "They're coming."

There was a clutching of weapons, a peering and listening. A deputy crouched beside the heap of oil-soaked waste, match ready.

The soft thudding slowed but did not cease, filtering through the moan and mutter of the swollen river. It seemed to hesitate as if in search of something, then continued as with renewed confidence. Another moment and shapes, grotesque, unreal in the starlight loomed, resolved to mounted men, seven in number. At the apex of the bend and directly opposite where the posse waited they pulled to a halt, the riders dismounted, turned toward the river bank. Slade could see that several carried shovels, and one a bundle wrapped in burlap, which he handled carefully. The Ranger's breath caught a little. If a slug hit that bundle! He leaned forward, touched the crouching deputy on the shoulder. There was a scratching sound, a tiny flicker, then a roar of flame shooting high in the air, making the scene momentarily bright as day.

The men who had started to climb the steep river bank whirled as Sheriff Cartwright's voice rang out, "In the name of the law! Elevate! You're covered!"

And as the burning waste flared higher, Slade recognized the tall form and handsome face, contorted with rage, of Gordon Plant.

But even as he glimpsed the cart train owner, Plant dodged behind a man beside him and fired over his shoulder, the bullet fanning Slade's face. His companions went for their guns and the night fairly exploded to the bellow of the reports.

Shooting with both hands, Slade tried to line sights with Plant, but the light from the burning waste was dimming and Plant was constantly on the move, ducking, dodging, weaving. Slade saw the outlaws falling, heard a yelp of pain behind him, a curse, and knew that a couple of the deputies had stopped lead. His own right sleeve was shot to ribbons, blood was streaming down his arm from where a slug had grazed the flesh. Dimly he saw a form flash toward. where the horses stood, and as he swung his guns around to bear, a deputy stumbled in front of him and he was forced to hold his fire. The next instant there was a thudding of fast hoofs and the shadowy form of a mounted man vanishing westward.

"It's Plant!" yelled Sheriff Cartwright. "He's getting away!"

And abruptly Slade realized there was nothing more in front to shoot at. He whirled and raced to where he had left Shadow.

"You fellers look after those hellions on the ground," the sheriff shouted to the deputies, and pounded after Slade, John Butler close on his heels.

"And somebody find that bundle of dynamite that's lying around somewhere," Slade called, as he flung himself into the saddle and scooped up the split reins. His voice rang out, "Trail, Shadow, trail!"

The black horse leaped forward and was going at flying

speed. Slade strained his eyes for a glimpse of the fugitive, and a moment later sighted his shadowy outline fully three hundred yards ahead. He urged Shadow to greater effort, for he saw that he had a race on his hands.

Plant was splendidly mounted. In the big sorrel he bestrode, Shadow had almost met his match. Almost, but not quite. Slowly, slowly he shortened the distance. Within a mile the three hundred yards of lead had shrunk to less than two, and the flying black was still gaining.

Far behind, hopelessly outdistanced but stubbornly hanging on, rode Sheriff Cartwright and John Butler.

Now Slade could make out the whitish blur of Plant's face as he turned to glare at his pursuer. He fingered the butt of his Winchester but reluctantly abandoned the idea. The light was very bad and to chance a shot at Plant he would have to sacrifice precious distance; and although he had every faith in Shadow, there was no guarantee that his endurance was as great as that of the powerful sorrel, who carried much the lighter load. Better to get a bit closer, even at the risk of stopping a slug himself when the showdown came.

The film of cloud over the stars was thickening, the light dimming even more. At the horses' very feet the river growled hungrily; but close to the water's edge was the only clear going free from tufts of brush and holes made by burrowing marmots. Slowly, slowly, Shadow closed the distance.

Abruptly Plant gave up the race. He jerked his mount to a halt, whirled him to face his pursuer and went for his guns. Weaving, ducking in the hull, Slade charged straight into the blaze of orange flame. Bullets whined past. One jostled his hat on his head. Another plucked urgently at his sleeve. Then his own Colts spurted fire and smoke. He saw Plant reel, steady himself, bring his guns to bear. Slade fired as fast as he could pull trigger, left, right, left, right. Now Shadow was almost shoulder to shoulder with the sorrel.

Plant screamed, a retching, rasping scream. He toppled, slumped, fell sideways from the hull, his body rolling over and over down the steep slope. A sullen plunge and, dead or dying, he vanished from sight forever.

Slade pulled to a halt and sat gazing at the swirling black water that was bearing what was left of Gordon Plant on his long, one-way journey to the sea.

TWENTY-TWO

HE WAS STILL SITTING THERE, gazing at the river, when Butler and Cartwright pulled their foaming horses to a halt beside him.

"Did you get him?" the sheriff asked anxiously.

"I'm not sure," Slade replied, his voice listless, "but I am sure for certain that the Rio Grande did."

"Good!" growled Cartwright. "Wanted to turn the water loose, eh? Well, he can help himself to all he wants, now. You all right?"

"Right arm scratched a little, nothing to pay any mind to," Slade answered. "Let's get back to the boys and see how they made out. Bring his horse along. It's a good one and he won't be needing it anymore."

Torches were flickering as they drew near the scene of battle, and by their light they saw five bodies laid out in a row. A glance told Slade that one was Clate Erwin, Plant's carting boss.

"Anybody badly hurt?" he asked, as he dismounted.

"Just a couple of nicks—I took care of 'em," replied Radcliff, the chief deputy. "We got one of the hellions alive—hole through his shoulder. I held up the blood as best I could with a couple of handkerchiefs and the tail of my shirt. Maybe he'll make it."

They bent over the wounded man, a slightly built, thin-faced individual with bright intelligent eyes. Butler let out an astounded bellow, *"Quigley!"*

"Yes, Quigley," the other gasped.

"Why in blazes—" Butler began, but Slade stopped him with a gesture.

"I want to have a look at the wound before he talks," he said. "In my left saddle pouch you'll find a roll of bandage and a jar of antiseptic salve. Fetch them, please."

Butler did as he was told. Slade removed Radcliff's makeshift dressing and examined the bullet puncture. It was still bleeding somewhat but there were no bubbles to indicate a wind wound; evidently the slug missed the lung. He went to work on the injury and soon had the bleeding under control, and the injured member padded and bandaged. He rolled and lighted a cigarette and put it between Quigley's lips. The engineer inhaled gratefully and smiled wanly at his benefactor.

124

"And now, if there's anything you'd like to tell us—" Slade suggested gently.

"Not much to tell," Quigley replied, with a bitter smile. "Plant, who was a hatchet-man for the M.K., got hold of me and led me in. I was desperate for money, a lot of it. My wife was very ill, badly in need of an operation I felt might save her. It didn't; she died."

"If you'd only gone to Mr. Dunn with your troubles," Slade said sadly. "He would have helped you."

"I thought of it—too late," Quigley answered wearily. "Plant got complete control of me, of course, and I had to do as he said."

"Like planning the bridge where it would be sure to go out with the first bad flood," Slade observed.

"That's right," Quigley agreed. "And he got completely *out* of control so far as the M.K. people were concerned. He was shrewd and had gotten hold of letters and papers, the contents of which they didn't want revealed, to put it mildly. So they couldn't stop him when he began doing things they wouldn't have condoned. He got scared when you showed up and discovered the planned error of the bridge, and he seemed to go absolutely *loco* and would stop at nothing. Would you roll me another cigarette, please?"

Slade did so. Quigley took a couple of deep drags and continued, "As you doubtelss know, the M.K. people paid for his ranch, to be used largely as a cover-up, and helped him get started in the carting business after the bridge deal was put over."

"I guessed as much," Slade admitted. "The carting business will always be a paying proposition, plenty of business from outlying sections even after the railroad goes through. Then they'll run to Ojinaga across the river instead of heading on north via the Chihuahua. Go on."

"He was also to receive a large sum of money contingent on the C. & P. being delayed long enough to let the M.K. reach Chihuahua City first."

"Naturally," Slade agreed. "And I suppose Plant kept a tight hold on you?"

"Yes, I've been a virtual prisoner ever since my bridge survey was accepted. I didn't want to come here tonight, but he forced me to because I'd know best to set the explosives to blow out the river bank."

"A hefty bundle of the stuff, too," Radcliff interpolated. "We got it safe."

"Any more of his bunch running around loose?" Slade

asked. Quigley drew hard on his cigarette and shook his head.

"Don't think so," he replied. "With the two cowhands and the two carters you did in tonight, I think the bunch is wiped out. Not all his cowboys or carters were in on the deal. You killed two of his cowhands who tried to attack the wagon train. That scared the devil out of him, but he managed to spirit away the bodies before they were taken to Presidio, where they would have been recognized as Barred Diamond hands. Yes, I think the whole outfit is wiped out."

"And a blankety-blank good thing," growled Sheriff Cartwright. "Now what, Walt?"

"Guess we'd better be getting back to town and see how the bridge is coming along. I think you can ride, Quigley, and—don't worry too much." He smiled down at the little engineer, his cold eyes abruptly compassionate and understanding. Quigley drew a deep breath, winced at the pain it caused him but looked greatly relieved.

"Nominally you are a prisoner in the sheriff's custody, but I don't think he need worry about you trying to run away," Slade added.

"I'm through running for the rest of my life," Quigley declared vigorously.

"Dunn will never prosecute him," Slade confided to the sheriff as they rode in the rear of the group. "He'll straighten him out and find him employment; he does things like that. And I aim to get Dunn and Andy Jorg together, too. They didn't make out so well the first time they met, but now, working together they can do a great deal of good for the section."

"I think," chuckled the sheriff, "that you could talk wolves and lambs into layin' down peaceful together. Say! come to think of it, you didn't seern at all surprised when we turned up Quigley."

"I wasn't," Slade admitted. "I'd just been wondering where and when we would turn him up. Remember the plat of the river, that I took off the little snake who tried to blow up the powder house? He was an expert powder man and his next chore was to blow the riverbank and let the water onto the lowlands. Well, I knew that plat was drawn by an engineer, and I didn't think Plant was an engineer. So it was logical to believe that he had Quigley holed up somewhere within reach, and that the chore of blowing the bank would be turned over to him after the other fellow was out of the running. See?"

126

Sheriff Cartwright shook his head in wordless admiration.

In the gray light of dawn, the last ponderous girder thudded into place. The frustrated Rio Grande growled and grumbled angrily and frothed against the masonry, but the pier, in solid foundation on the eternal rock of earth, stood scornfully aloof, as much as to say, "Beller all you want to and see how much good it'll do you! I'll run a thousand million tons of freight across your lousy back!"

And onto the approach boomed a big locomotive hauling a single green and gold private car. Jaggers Dunn made it for the finish!

Later, Jaggers chortled from time to time as he listened to the story Slade had to tell.

"And there's your bridge, days ahead of schedule," the Ranger concluded. "What else is to be done is just a routine chore. I trust you won't object to the bonus I promised the boys."

"We'll just double it," grunted the G.M.

"I know there's no use trying to get you to accept anything," he added, "but here's a little contribution to the fund you had set up to help dependents of rangers killed in the line of duty."

Slade's lips pursed in a soundless whistle as he read the amount of the General Manager's check.

"And," said Dunn, "I'm sending a little wire to the M.K. folks at their New York office. Nothing controversial, just in the nature of a news item." Slade chuckled as he read,

> WE HAVE POTTER QUIGLEY SAFE
> IN JAIL. HE TALKED.

"That should keep them off your back for a while, I'd say," Slade smiled.

"So I figure," grinned Dunn. "And now what?"

"Now I'm going to spend a few days at the Barred Diamond ranchhouse, then I'm heading for the Post to see what Captain Jim has lined up for me," Slade replied. "But I'll be back down here soon to look things over."

Three days later, Mary Nellis and Andy Jorg watched him ride away, his eyes aglow with the promise of duty, danger, and new adventure. At the bend of the trail, he called back, *"Hasta luego!* Till we meet again!"